RETURN TO KALYMNOS

Andrea Stallan

Copyright © 2020 Andrea Stallan

All rights reserved

The characters and events portrayed in this book are fictitious. Any similarity to real persons, living or dead, is coincidental and not intended by the author.

No part of this book may be reproduced, or stored in a retrieval system, or transmitted in any form or by any means, electronic, mechanical, photocopying, recording, or otherwise, without express written permission of the publisher.

ISBN 9798677603778

Cover © Shutterstock

*A huge thanks to my family and friends
for their patience and contributions!*

Chapter 1

So many memories. I closed the door to 23 Belmont Close for the last time.

'Where are you off to?'

'Greece,' I reply.

'Love it there, go every year,' he says.

Out of nowhere heavy rain pounds against the car windows.

'Where do you stay?' I ask.

'Makrigialos, been going with the missus for the last ten years. Thought about moving out there for good, but she won't leave the grandkids. How long are you going for?'

I pause for a moment, the reality now very real. Meeting his eyes in the rear view mirror. 'It's my new home.'

He doesn't respond, just a nod of his head.

My cases are lifted from the boot of his car and I open my purse to pay.

'That won't be necessary my love. You have a fantastic life,' he says.

Tears well up in my eyes. 'Thank you.'

I walk towards the departure sign.

My first visit to the island happened twenty years ago. It was almost the end of July and the abundance of sunshine promised never actually materialised. So, on a rainy afternoon we found ourselves booking a last minute holiday, our first together, we'd been seeing each other for six months.

I had gone to a house party with my best friend Clare and soon after arriving a guy called Steve began chatting her up, forcing me to stand by like a gooseberry. It wasn't an uncommon scenario, Clare was supremely confident with the opposite sex, the way she posed, the eye contact she gave them as if performing on a stage. I wouldn't say I was shy back then, probably pickier than Clare and often left to make my own way home after a night out with her.

A good-looking guy with brown wavy hair appeared, in each hand a bottle of beer. He looked at Steve, raised his eyes to the ceiling and handed a bottle to me.

'Paul,' he said tapping his bottle against mine.

'Kate,' I replied.

I noticed Paul's cheeky smile as we chatted, to go with his looks and I suppose you could say I was quite cute in my early twenties. My sandy coloured hair, long and curly. My frame petite. Although thinking back maybe I was a bit too generous with my application of black eyeliner!

It wasn't too long before I felt a tap on my shoulder. 'I'm leaving now,' Clare shouted into my ear.

'Already?'

A drunken grin her response. There was no doubt who with, she was a quick worker. To be honest, I wasn't annoyed by her departure. I had a new drinking partner and getting a good vibe from Paul, therefore in no rush to leave.

'Fancy a dance,' Paul asked.

'Okay.' And he grabbed my hand and led me to the centre of the living room to join others.

Paul moved his hips to the beat of the song and impressed me with his rhythm. He took both my hands and turned me expertly around, neither of us submitting as song after song played. Eventually we collapsed on to a huge brown sofa and we had our first kiss. And kissed for a long time.

I remember opening my eyes and first light seeping through between poorly fitted purple curtains. The sight and smell of alcohol induced bodies littered the room and then the beginning of a thumping head as it rested on another's shoulder. As I looked up my eyes met Paul's and he was smiling at me. I smiled back, resting my head for a little longer.

The fresh cold winter air engulfed our bodies as we shuffled out amongst the other party stragglers. They soon disappeared out of sight leaving me and Paul alone. Then came an awkward moment, did we kiss again or hug our farewell. I was secretly praying for the latter, my mouth crying out for my teeth and tongue to be cleaned.

'Are you going to give me your number then?' he asked. In no doubt I wanted to see him again, and hoped he wasn't asking for my number because it seemed the right thing to do. I suspect we have all met a few in our time; the ones that have no real intention of following through. Thinking back I'm relieved some of them didn't make contact. On this occasion I couldn't wait for Paul's call and didn't have to wait long.

Paul's local travel agent tapped away on the keyboard, with an occasional shake of his head. We sat patiently.

'How about this one, an unnamed resort deal to the Greek Island of Kos leaving tomorrow night,' Ian finally said.

'What type of accommodation is it?' Paul asked.

'It isn't specified, that is why it's called a deal.'

He looked at Paul as if he were stupid and realising the error of his way smiled. 'But don't worry you are almost certain to be holidaying in one of the popular resorts such as Kos Town. The hotels and apartments are a good standard there, I've been myself.'

Ian promptly sprang from his seat to take a brochure from the neatly stacked shelves behind him. Flicking through and finding the correct page, he presented the sun-baked island. Neither of us had been to Greece before, desperate to get some sun we took his word for it.

No time to do a holiday shop, I thought I could buy new clothes when I arrived there. For a week, I doubted I would need much anyhow. We nearly didn't make it all, Paul couldn't find his passport and eventually found it in a secret compartment in his suitcase. Then we got stuck in traffic and just arrived to the boarding area in time, the last passengers to take seats on the plane. You know the ones I'm talking about.

As we exited the building at Kos airport, we met with a rush of intense heat. Soon after I spotted a blonde haired woman dressed in a bright yellow suit, waiving a clip board above her head. In her Geordie accent, she informed our small gathering that our accommodation was on the island of Kalymnos, not a place either of us had heard of. We needed to get on a ferry to take us there, along with the other travellers who appeared as surprised as us. Had we all booked the same cheap deal crossed my mind.

In the blazing sun, we set off on the next leg of our journey by sea, managing to find partially shaded seats on the top deck, a gentle sea breeze attempting to cool our overheated bodies.

Thirty minutes later we arrived at our destination. Suitcases were discarded on the stone quayside in a disorderly fashion and a lot of huffing and puffing pursued from our fellow holidaymakers, not the best way to start a holiday.

Having no idea what to do next, it soon became apparent that our travel rep had not taken the boat journey with us. Someone spotted a number of taxi drivers lined up close by, each driver holding a sign displaying a hand written name.

We climbed in our car and I suspected this was an early clue we weren't holidaying in a busy resort. And to be honest this wasn't an issue for me, I was spending a whole week with Paul.

Our driver appeared to be in a hurry, taking corners wildly and with such speed that we collided into each other on the shiny black vinyl seats. The car filled with cigarette smoke, the driver lighting one after another and us sharing a look 'What are we doing here?' It was a huge relief when he dropped us off and we climbed the stairs to our apartment.

I remember entering and being hit with an overwhelming vision of sky blue. In fact all of the furniture happened to be blue, from a tired dressing table to the mirror frame hung on the wall and not forgetting the walls. There was no balcony, only a small square window that looked out on to barren land.

'There's no pool,' I said.

Paul wrapped his arms around me and sensing my disappointment teased me towards one of the single beds.

According to the single sheet of paper left for us, at most ten lines, there didn't appear to be a lot happening near our apartment. Paul thought it would be a good idea for us to hire a moped for the day.

'It will be fun and we will get to see more of the island this way,' he said. I willingly obliged even though I had no idea if he had ridden one before. You throw yourself into situations when you are young and don't think about what could possibly go wrong.

The following day, armed with a map provided by the owner of the shop we set off. We had only been travelling for ten minutes when we made our first pit stop. Paul laid the map on the table.

'Let's head to the capital, Pothia,' he said taking a swig of his beer. 'Bound to be loads to see there.' And I agreed.

No helmets provided back then, and a combination of the blistering sun baking the tops of our heads, coupled with another beer en route was making my head fuzzy. I felt relieved when we arrived in Pothia and took refuge in the *Monastry of Agnos Savvas*. It sat perched on top of a hill in prime position, overlooking the town.

Our visit brief, I got a bout of hiccups out of nowhere, followed by a fit of giggles and Paul had to usher me out. Too embarrassed to set foot back inside, we hopped back on the moped.

A few hours spent wandering around the capital, including a late lunch, followed with a scrumptious ice cream and then a stroll on the beach and an unplanned dip in the sea (no cozzies, just underwear), the day flew by. We hadn't anticipated how long it would take us to get back and as the sun faded the skies grew darker. Paul decided to take a short cut, confident he was taking the right road back until it soon turned into a dirt track enclosed by trees. I held on tight as the track got steeper and rockier as Paul tried to navigate the large uneven stones on our path. I was convinced we were going to get a puncture and have to camp out under the blackness of the night sky, but kept my thoughts to myself. The idea of sleeping under the stars with my boyfriend sounded romantic for a moment, until I imagined the creatures who would have their piece of us, flying and otherwise.

By some miracle, we eventually arrived back and found the owner standing outside his shop as

Paul brought the bike to a standstill. The Greek man stood with his arms crossed and his jaw clenched, looking not too pleased with us or the state of the bike we were returning. I tried to stifle my laugh while Paul was apologising. His charm not working on this occasion.

We drank a lot that holiday I recall - one particular night we got extremely drunk. We had been for a drink near our apartment and then headed down to the seafront, in search for more life there. We came across a bright red sign directing us to take downward stairs and as we ventured down, the bar appeared to be built inside a cave. We found the place practically empty but we sat at a table next to a local man.

'English?' Keen to strike up a conversation, he began to ask us questions, where we were from, which football team we supported, and the usual chit chat. He offered to buy us a drink, so we ordered a couple of beers and another drink in a small glass appeared on the table. The local man had this other drink placed in front of him too.

'Yamas,' he said and knocked his drink back. He reminded me of the Laughing Buddha with his bald head and wide smile. He raised his hand upwards and we assumed he wanted us to knock our drink back too, therefore we followed suit.

The clear liquid tasted sweet similar to

peaches, quite sickly as it hit my taste buds. We drank our beer and Paul decided to return the compliment and buy our newly acquainted friend the same sickly drink back, along with more beer. Unfortunately this act of kindness continued into the night and I lost count of how many drinks we shared. I tried to get Paul to leave with a few glances and a nod of my head towards the exit, but he was in his element laughing and joking, cheekily smiling back at me. I reluctantly gave up trying to persuade him and drank everything put in front of me. It wasn't until later during a game of darts (most of mine didn't hit the board) that we found out our drinking buddy owned the bar. A brilliant tactic, he clearly didn't pay for his drinks and we suspected we weren't the first holidaymakers he used this trick on. Let's just say we felt very hung over the following day and succumbed to a lazy day in the shade.

When the end of our week arrived, I didn't want to leave the island. That dreaded sensation in the pit of your stomach when the realisation hits; you have to return to work. We laughed recalling our memories on the flight home and every now and then I glanced down at the shiny silver ring on my right hand, a holiday gift from Paul.

What did I like about Paul? Everything. You know when you have met the one.

Chapter 2

'Probably died instantly,' they said.

Paul died three years ago. I still can't comprehend he has gone. He was on his way home from work, the familiar journey he'd taken so many times before when the fatal crash occurred. My husband, the man I loved with all my being, cruelly taken from me. Our dreams and plans erased in an instant. Our bubble had burst and my body wasn't prepared for such catastrophic news. First the numbness and then blackness.

Paul died on a Monday and I went back to my job the following Monday. Too soon? Most definitely, but I didn't want to stay at home. Was I depressed? Of course. Was I present? Absolutely not as I managed to get through my work tasks without conversing unless I had to. My first day back nobody spoke to me, apart from a quick welcome back from my manager who was dashing to a meeting and only one other person. Simon sat behind me, he didn't speak much, focused on his work and not known for mingling.

Simon sidled his chair up to mine on that first day. 'Nobody knows what to say.' He gave me a reassuring smile. 'Same happened when my mum died.'

It made sense, people weren't being unkind they didn't want to upset me. I vaguely remembered Simon's mum's death and felt ashamed I hadn't spoken to him to check he was okay. I guess I assumed at the time, it was better to carry on as normal around those that have lost.

Getting use to doing everyday activities is a struggle when your other half isn't beside you, it is tough and nothing, I repeat nothing, can prepare you for the biggest climb of your life. Writing became my saviour, taking me away from a daily fog of grief which seemed to linger. It gave me an avenue to escape from the darkness of despair. When I couldn't face social interaction, I felt a sense of control and escapism when I began to write. It was my therapy and has become so much more to me.

Slowly I came to realise I needed to start afresh, a second chance, something completely different and somewhere with guaranteed sunshine appealed to me. That is why for the last eight months

I have lived here on the island of Kalymnos. It is situated between the better known islands of Kos and Leros, perhaps you have heard of Kalymnos or holidayed here?

I guess you could say I fell on my feet. With my affairs seen to, including the sale of our house, didn't take long. I felt excited, fuelled by an abundance of energy as my plan gathered pace. Before I took the plunge to move here I did consider other options, but found myself drawn back to this island, as if I had unfinished business here. I looked forward to not knowing what lay in store.

I made a couple of short visits on my own to Kalymnos, keeping my secret from friends and family in case they tried to talk me out of it. 'Are you mad?' 'You will get lonely.' 'Is it safe?' All the questions and statements I expected when I told them my life changing news. Luckily I came across a small house similar to a cottage in England, the owner keen to sell quickly, it had been empty for three months.

As soon as I saw the house I fell in love with it straight away. It sat in an isolated spot, no other houses in sight as far as I could see, but needing a bit of attention, well quite a lot actually. The once white painted exterior appeared quite shabby in places where brown brick work showed through. Royal blue shutters protected the windows, some sitting at awkward angles. I followed the silver haired male agent through a blue door, framed in a simple arch as we began the viewing.

Once inside, the interior walls looked as equally unloved, where pictures of different shapes and sizes had hung on their faded canvas. Considering the heat outside, the air inside felt cool against my skin as the agent showed the ground floor area: a kitchen and living room combined, perfect for one. A wooden staircase a little creaky underfoot took us to a master bedroom and a smaller bedroom, a single bed left behind. A room ideal for storing I noted and finally the bathroom, floor to ceiling covered in black and white tiles, basic, though in full working order. Any jobs that needed doing not an issue, I presumed I would have plenty of time to get around to them. I had already made my mind up about the house before being taken out to view the garden, which also needed some loving care. I didn't hesitate to make an offer, I knew this house was for me.

On the 1st January I arrived. A new year, new life and new me. The first few weeks were taken up with unpacking boxes and cleaning down surfaces. It was hard going, though not unmanageable and dare I say therapeutic at times. Furthermore, it made my move more real and not just a holiday let. I found evidence of the previous owners in cupboards, a wooden spoon left behind in a drawer and a clock that had stopped mounted on the kitchen wall. Had they left in a hurry? I should have asked the agent more about the previous owners, for all I knew something serious could have happened in the house itself. I didn't spot any obvious signs; blood stains or bullet holes. Probably best not to know just in case, I didn't want to jinx my new abode.

I love my house with its rustic charm and after a short stroll you can find fantastic views of the coastline and shimmering Aegean Sea. And of course endless days of cloudless blue sky to look forward to. What more could you ask for.

That's me, happy and content. Sounds boring? As if I could get quite lonely.

So, let me introduce you to my new friends...

Chapter 3

The day after I arrived, I was on my way into the local town when the heavens opened. I hadn't brought an umbrella to the island and this was clearly an oversight, it was January after all. Luckily, the dome shaped orange roof enticed me towards the church.

I stood in the doorway taking shelter, wiping the rain from my face, concluding this wasn't going to be a quick shower by the greyness of the sky. I leaned back against the wooden door, it opened. Intrigued to find out what lay inside, I ventured in.

The cool air engulfed my skin and my body shivered in response. I glanced around, no sign of human life. I sat on one of the wooden benches towards the back of the church and closed my eyes, breathing in deeply and exhaling. A peacefulness took over my body, a trancelike state and I was surprised to discover this sudden sense of calmness I hadn't experienced before.

When I eventually opened my eyes to my surprise someone sat to the left of me. They must have crept in and I felt alarmed why someone would sit so close in an empty church. I didn't panic. From the corner of my eye I slowly took in the sight of this person and acknowledged a man and he was clearly attired in priest garments. I gradually turned my head to the left to find he had jet black hair and dark brown eyes which met with mine. I managed a faint smile unsure what to do next, my deep breathing now replaced by a quicker pace. A moment of awkwardness until he spoke first and introduced himself.

'I'm Nicolaos.' That was all he said.

'I'm Kate.' That was all I said.

And then loud footsteps of someone entering the church. Another man. He approached us and spoke in Greek to the priest sitting beside me. So I seized the opportunity to hurry myself out of the sacred place, back through the wooden door, relieved to find the rain had finally stopped.

On my way home I'm ashamed to say I thought about the priest with the jet black hair and dark brown eyes. He looked a similar age to me and an extremely handsome man.

A week had passed by before I visited the church,

hoping to find my inner calmness again and perhaps a chance meeting with the priest called Nicolaos. On this occasion the handsome priest did not appear to be inside, instead I was presented with a fatter, older priest with an untidy grey beard. He nodded his head to me as I entered. My expectation unfulfilled and after five minutes I promptly departed. Stupid really when I gave thought to it, I had only met the man, correction priest once and what did I think was going to happen?

I had work to do, the first draft of my book was due with my literary agent in four months' time. My agent is called Janet. She is a lively character and unlike anyone I'd ever met in my previous work environment. It is worth explaining that I worked in Finance before I started to write seriously, a strange choice of profession you may think considering I studied History at University. Which incidentally I loved studying, but wasn't sure what to do with a History degree when I graduated. I was also good at Maths, which is why I ended up working with figures. Deep down though, I realised I didn't want a life time career of balancing spreadsheets, writing yet another strategic report and sitting in countless boring meetings. Day in day out, having to observe the other frustrated faces who were probably thinking the same as me. After Paul's death, it spurred me into action to become what I really wanted to be: a writer. Life is too short as the saying goes and I certainly had experience of that.

Sitting in the hairdressers one day, flicking through a magazine, I read a short story. While there my 'light bulb' moment occurred and I thought why not. So, I wrote a short story and sent it off to the same magazine and they published it. Shortly after its publication I received an unexpected phone call from Janet. I had no idea how she obtained my number, and she told me with enthusiasm, that she thoroughly enjoyed my story and believed I had potential. I was buzzing after this feedback, not expecting anything would come from my first piece of writing.

Janet suggested we meet for lunch the following week; a restaurant chosen by her in the centre of London. As the date grew closer I played out the meeting in my head and did some research about Janet's work. Janet's picture on her website implied she was probably in her early sixties. Her silver hair pearlescent, cut into a short youthful style and the frames of her glasses bright red to match her lipstick. As I read several pieces about her, I felt reassured when I found she had represented a decent number of people spanning twenty years.

On the day of our meeting, Janet's spirited and intellectual persona was infectious and we hit it off straight away. We covered all sorts of subjects as we chatted, ably assisted by the fact both of us partial to a glass of red wine.

A few weeks after we met, Janet invited me to a book launch. 'A taste of what to expect,' she said. It was an evening event in London, therefore I needed to book an overnight stay. I asked what I should wear and Janet told me it wouldn't be cocktail dresses, something smart but not fussy. I felt a bit out of my depth when I came off the phone, worrying about what I should wear and I wouldn't know anyone there.

When the day of the book launch arrived, I began to feel nervous. After checking into my hotel, I changed into a plain black dress and long boots with a moderate sized heel and a poncho with a faux fur collar to finish my outfit, prepared for a chilly autumnal night. I took out my notebook finding the address of the event and grabbed a taxi to the Art Gallery in Shoreditch.

Walking through the door I noticed most people were dressed more casually, some even in jeans, as I tugged on the hem of my poncho. A waiter arrived by my side balancing fluted glasses on a silver tray and I didn't hesitate to take one to settle my nerves. This a world I wasn't familiar in.

Apart from artwork displayed on the white walls, a small stage had been set up for the reader and at most fifty chairs. Janet was nowhere in sight and I was beginning to wonder if she'd made it.

'Please take your seats,' said a soothing male voice.

A woman with short black curly hair stepped onto the stage and I quickly found a seat as the lights dimmed. The authors name was Grace Rodgers and she sat on the lone chair and reached for the glass set beside her. She took a sip of the water (I assumed it to be) as we sat patiently for her to begin. I looked down at my empty glass disappointed, wondering if there would be more champagne flowing.

Janet hadn't told me anything about the author or what her novel was about, all very intriguing. Grace surveyed the audience, took a moment and began. 'I lay numb in the freezing cold and couldn't see her face .....' Grace's story held my attention from the off, the hairs on my arms standing on end. If she was nervous I couldn't tell as she read two chapters with poise.

No sooner than the lights brightened, Janet appeared by my side. I had no idea where she'd been, although later she told me she missed her tube and managed to sneak in during the second chapter. Janet was Grace's agent and I was invited to the post launch meal along with a select few. I was keen to talk to Grace, hopeful she could give me some tips.

Janet made sure that Grace sat between us two as we seated ourselves within a large half mooned shaped booth in an Italian restaurant. As we chatted I couldn't quite believe how such a warm and charming lady like Grace could write incredibly disturbing scenes. I found Grace extremely generous with her experience of writing a first novel as I asked more and more questions with the flow of wine. I hoped I would remember it all.

Janet rooted around in her oversized handbag while we waited for my taxi and eventually took out a silver compact mirror to reapply her trademark red lipstick.

'Did you enjoy tonight?' she asked pursing her lips into a pout.

'I did, thank you Janet for inviting me,' I replied blowing warm air into my chilled hands.

'This could be you in a few years' time, believe in yourself,' Janet said, her eyebrows raised above the red frames of her glasses.

I had delivered a number of presentations at work during my time. I wasn't confident I would ever be able to pull off a public reading though, however didn't want to contradict Janet or question her judgement, after all she was the expert. Consequently I have Janet to thank for giving me the courage to take the plunge and write my first proper novel and finally leave my job.

I busied myself in my writing and tried not to think of the handsome priest called Nicolaos.

Chapter 4

I had gone to the local market in the square to buy a few provisions and just finished bargaining (which I was still mastering), for fresh fruit and vegetables. I remember the first time I ventured to the market, the sound of spoken Greek words an alien language to me. My sense of smell awoken to aromas, some sweet, others fragrant filling the air. I watched as locals pointed and gestured before they committed themselves. I didn't buy anything that day, not wanting to embarrass myself and instead memorised the scene and what was being sold, ready for when I returned.

That all seems a distant memory to how at ease I feel now when I visit the market. I enjoy the game of bartering with the locals, it is a part of my new life.

He had his back to me but definitely him, his

garments and thick black hair a sure giveaway. He appeared surprisingly tall too, of course I wouldn't have presumed this as we were sitting during our first encounter.

I delved into my shabby leather purse, its crinkled leather showing the sign of its age and moved towards another stall on the market selling freshly baked bread. I didn't need any. I glanced around and he was walking in my direction and I was suddenly conscious of smoothing down my hair. It is naturally curly and the heat seems to encourage this further, most of the time it is tied back in a casual fashion. But not this day.

I chose a rustic looking bread and opened my purse to pay.

'It is a beautiful day,' he said in a deep voice, a few steps away from me.

I straightened my posture before I turned around.

He was even taller close up compared to my five foot two frame. 'It is,' I replied my mouth forming a smile.

He raised his right hand. 'I am walking back to the church, let me help you.' He glanced down towards the bags in my hands.

'I'm fine.' How did he know I had finished buying and that I was walking his way?

'Please,' he said.

I accepted his kind offer and we walked away from the market at a slow pace (which surprised me with his long legs). I looked around a couple of times and wondered if anybody was watching us. The locals appeared to be friendly therefore we probably didn't seem out of place, apart from an obvious height difference. It wouldn't have surprised me to find he offered to do this for other people too. I hoped this to be the case and it wasn't out of pity for me.

The familiar tranquil walk back led us via a winding road, passing an olive grove and then up a small incline to the church. It was another five minutes' walk to my house from there.

'Thank you,' I said, 'let me take those from you.' I assumed he would be needed back at his church to do God's work.

He moved his head from side to side and pointed forward, I carried on walking towards my house. Strange I thought, how he knew the way and in no time at all our journey together ended.

'Goodbye,' he said and turned to walk away. I thought it odd he didn't have anything else to say.

'Wait,' my voice louder than I intended. Nicolaos turned back.

'Would you like some tea?'

'Tea would be good Kate.' Surprised he remembered my name. Then quickly concluded he was unlikely to meet anyone else called Kate.

I steered Nicolaos along the narrow path at the side of my house to the garden while I popped the food inside and prepared tea for my guest. I brought a decent supply of English breakfast tea to the island hoping the comfort of its traditional brew would help me settle in. However, when I began to run out I had taken to buying from the market. It appeared Greek people grew their own, Chamomile a popular choice.

And there we sat at the small round weathered table in my garden, looking out over the rugged landscape dotted with random bushes and trees. When I say garden, it is really a plot of unkempt scorched grass surrounded by a low and uneven stone wall. Three large terracotta pots sat on the paved patio area, filled with unrecognisable plants, here when I moved in. They looked passed revivable. Even the stray dogs didn't venture into my garden!

I felt an edginess at first, having never spoken to a priest before, definitely not socially and in fact come to think of it, not at all. We didn't have a church wedding, deciding on a local hotel to tie the knot. And Paul wanted a humanist funeral, not that he had written a Will, just something he'd stated, therefore no need to talk to the local church vicar. Paul's service was held at the Crematorium and a male humanist spoke about the man I had lost forever. It felt surreal. I wasn't sure what I was supposed to feel. I'd imagined I would be a gibbering wreck, but nothing poured out of me. The wake followed at our local pub and honestly I can't remember much about it. Firstly, I was still in denial Paul was no longer around and secondly, I drank copious amounts of alcohol which were continually thrust into my hand. To this day I have absolutely no idea how or with whom I got home.

Paul's ashes were finally parked on the window ledge in our kitchen after a spell in our bedroom, the living room and even the bathroom, waiting to be scattered as I had no idea what to do with them. That was until I came to live on Kalymnos and his ashes travelled with me. I did get some strange glances from other passengers when I handed over the urn, non-metallic of course to allow for screening. And I had to provide his death certificate and a statement from the crematorium confirming the contents. All proper and correct procedure to stop drug smuggling I presumed. Did I fit the typical description of a drug smuggler? Possibly, in recent times women travellers had been used and caught out.

I fiddled with my wedding ring which without doubt I still wore, wondering what I could talk to a priest about. I guessed most people talked about their problems or confessed their sins, neither came to mind in that moment. What an interesting profession, I was curious if any priests had written their memoirs. Perhaps they were required to sign some kind of confidentiality agreement or something?

I had nothing to worry about, I was over thinking. I told Nicolaos of how I found myself living on the island and how my love for it began. It is said that time is a great healer and thankfully I didn't get upset when I retold my cherished memories of Paul.

Nicolaos listened patiently with an occasional movement of his head, which you would expect in his line of work and then disclosed some information about his life. His English very good as he spoke, an even pace leaving natural gaps between words. I learnt that his father was Greek and his mother Turkish; quite a combination. Nicolaos was originally from Athens, his parents still lived there and he was one of three sons. His eldest brother a doctor, worked in a hospital and the younger one a lawyer. He told me he had asked to come to Kalymnos but did not disclose why. I suspected there may be more to this story but didn't want to pry.

Our conversation came to a natural stop. Nicolaos stood, declaring he was needed at the church. He thanked me for the tea (which he barely touched) and before he departed he turned to me.

'Kate, you can call me Nico.'

The following week I met Nico again at the market, we just happened to bump into each other. I had two full bags of fruit and veg and Nico obviously concluded I needed help carrying them, so offered his services to assist me. I was quite capable of carrying my own shopping but I liked what appeared to be an unusual arrangement and presumed Nico did too.

On this occasion Nico asked if we could stop by the church as he had something he needed to collect. Not giving it too much thought, I waited for him by the small gate in front of the church. Soon after a man with a donkey approached, the animal's back covered in a red and black cloth where tools of a trade were strapped. The man waved to me as he passed by and I waved back.

When Nico reappeared he was carrying plants in an old wooden crate.

'For your garden.' Nico smiled, his teeth just visible and I couldn't help notice how white they appeared against the darkness of his skin.

'Thank you, that is very thoughtful of you Nico.' I think he felt sorry for me, as it was obvious for all to see I made no effort with my garden. In my defence it wasn't left in the best of states, still yet another job I needed to attend to. And it wasn't something I relished, in that I wasn't green fingered at all, and had no clue what the plants Nico carried were called and too embarrassed to ask.

There was another occasion when Nico surprised me with his kindness, I didn't make my weekly visit to the market and I guess he expected to see me. I felt a bit under the weather, no energy and stayed in bed drifting in and out of sleep. The following day when I opened my front door I found a basket of eggs. No note but I knew they were from him.

I took my seat and observed as Nico set about planting with the care they deserved, and then he joined me at the table. I had baked a lemon cake the day before, the island being plentiful of citrus fruits. It was one of the few I attempted in England, effortless to make and result pretty certain. Therefore no need for a recipe, I'd made it many times before. Paul loved it and Nico said he liked it and confirmed this by eating two pieces.

As Nico devoured the remains of his second piece, not a crumb left on his plate, I wondered if he were mindful about what he ate. My mind wandered and I thought about what his body looked like under his priest's garments. His chest smooth or hairy? If his body was tanned all over?

'Kate, it is delicious. Kate.' Nico brought me back to the here and now and I made some excuse I was daydreaming. Daydreaming indeed and clearly not appropriate behaviour.

And so our meets continued. I felt an urge to ask Nico more about himself, thinking if I offered him a glass of wine instead of tea, he might open up to me some more. I had no idea if priests were allowed to drink alcohol or if this was considered a sin. I wondered if Nico was allowed to eat out in a public place with a single woman. Technically a widowed woman, yet single all the same. Did he get lonely living on his own or maybe he received invites to other priest's houses for dinner? How many priests were there on our island? So many questions. This made our relationship all the more interesting in my eyes. I tried not to make it too obvious I found him to be an attractive man, though sometimes he caught me staring at him for a little longer than necessary.

Chapter 5

Now is a good time to tell you about Aella. I would guess her to be a couple of years younger than me and you could say she is typically Greek looking. Dark hair that she wears down mostly and falls softly upon her shoulders, big brown eyes which sit beneath naturally shaped brows and the sort of person you wouldn't forget in a hurry. She is a natural flirt with both sexes and is more than happy to be the centre of attention, unlike yours truly. You could see why her husband Stavros had fallen for her. Any man would.

I met Aella in the market, a few weeks after I'd arrived on the island. It came about while I was browsing and I spotted a vase, tall and elegant with white and black flowers painted on it. I became aware of a lady standing close to me, who also appeared to be admiring the vase in my hands and lingering for longer than I would have expected.

As I placed the vase to its original place I guessed that this Greek woman might be intrigued to know who I could be, though surprised when she invited me for coffee that day. 'We are going to get along fine,' she told me. We have been friends ever since and have naturally fallen into a routine of meeting for coffee and companionship. I cherish the vase she later bought as a gift for me.

It was around two months after meeting Aella, when I received an invite to a social occasion at her house she was hosting with Stavros. She mentioned it would be a few friends, some I had previously met and maybe some new faces from the local area.

On that morning I woke up early and drew back my bedroom curtains ready to revel in the incredible view. I found a man jogging past the house, wearing a baseball cap, shorts and t-shirt. I squinted to focus my sight and he didn't look Greek and then he disappeared quickly out of view. It wasn't a sight I expected and concluded he was probably somebody on holiday. I redirected my thoughts knowing I had got to a crucial scene in my writing, keen to get going.

I was ready for company having had a successful day writing. After a quick catch up with Aella, I made my way across the room to sit on a sumptuous black leather sofa and watched as people mingled in small groups. The buzz of Greek chatter filling the air. When I glanced down I was surprised how speedily I had emptied my glass.

I made my way to the table laden with different sized bottles of spirits and wine. I quickly located the bottle I last poured from and there was just enough to fill my glass with the dark red wine. As I looked up I spotted Stavros standing near the large window, conversing beside someone but my view was obscured. Stavros's laughter boomed across the room as he placed one of his hands on the person's shoulder the other raised upwards to emphasise his point. Stavros caught my stare and before I could look away he beckoned me over.

The fair haired man had his back to me.

'George, there is someone I would like you to meet,' Stavros said as I approached.

As he turned to face me, I registered a vague recollection. Stavros placed his arm around my shoulder.

'I'm George.' He held out his free hand to shake. The unexpected jogger.

'Kate.' I placed my hand in his.

He gave a hint of a smile and released my hand. He glanced down at the glass in his hand, swirling the ice around in a milky-white drink and I guessed he was drinking ouzo. Aella's voice carried across the room calling Stavros, his arm slipping from my shoulder.

'How do you know Stavros and Aella?' George asked and I couldn't help notice that his eyes were a sparkling green. I'd never met anyone with eyes like his before.

'I am a friend of Aella's, well both of them really, but more Aella,' I rattled out with speed.

He lifted his glass to his lips.

'And you?' I asked.

George didn't get a chance to reply, Stavros returned from being summoned by Aella. And I didn't get chance to ask my question again, we were joined by other people.

It left me wondering how George knew Stavros and Aella and why they hadn't mentioned him before. To my knowledge, I was their only English friend living in our town and maybe the whole island.

The following day I settled down to start writing early, after breakfast which usually consists of fruit smothered in yogurt and coffee to kick start my brain. I try to write in short spurts, usually an hour at a time depending on how my creative juices are flowing. Being new to the writing process I wasn't certain this was the best approach, still it appeared to be working for me.

Around midmorning, I rewarded myself with a break. I splashed on sun cream, grabbed my sunhat from the table inside the front door and headed out. I took a wander down to the sea before the midday rays became too hot for an English rose like me. We were having an unusually warm April according to Aella and being fair skinned and prone to the odd freckle I am sensible in the sun. Unlike my younger self.

When I look out across the glistening sea, taking in my beautiful surroundings and feel endless warmth on my skin, I have to pinch myself. I often imagined Paul standing beside me, my hand in his and close my eyes and hear the familiar tone of his voice. I talk to him, keeping him up to date with my new life, I know it sounds foolish but somehow makes his loss less painful and keeps him alive.

I ventured down further to the water's edge, kicking off my well-worn leather sandals and let the cool shallow water cover my toes and ankles. I glanced down regarding my feet and the idea of treating them to a pedicure sprang to mind, but I had no idea where I would find such a service. Then again, I was confident Aella would know of a place. My musings were interrupted by the sound of a car close by.

Twisting my body around, I looked up, but with the sun shining brightly into my eyes I couldn't make out who it was.

'Hello there,' somebody shouted. A man's voice.

Whoever he was, he got out of the car and then I recognised him. George stepped over the small wall and made his way down to me, my feet still planted in the sea. He approached in a crisp white shirt and khaki trousers and I noticed his brown shoes too, exceptionally shiny. Must have been due to the military conditioning I later found out about.

George tilted his sunglasses so that his eyes were just visible. 'Gorgeous morning isn't it?' His voice upbeat and realising the sunshine was too bright returned the dark frames to their rightful place.

'Yes it is,' I replied. Then again most mornings were.

'I've got a flat tyre, must be a puncture.'

'Oh that's bad luck.' I hoped he wasn't coming to ask me to help him.

'Did you enjoy the party Kate?'

I moved out of the water without drawing attention to my needy feet.

'Yes I did.'

'My head's a bit sore, had a few too many Ouzos,' George said, massaging his head.

I nodded in recognition as I suspected he left long after me. I wasn't sure who should speak next as we both stood.

Thankfully he spoke. 'Anyway, best get going and get this tyre changed. Bye Kate.'

'Bye George,' I replied and smiled.

And he turned and walked back to his car. I still had no further information about George and somewhat intrigued to know more about him. Where had he been hiding since I moved to the island? I debated whether to head back myself although that would mean passing George, or staying put. I decided to stay put until he left, assuming the task of changing a tyre didn't take too long.

George departed fifteen minutes later and I had a raging thirst.

I repeated the same routine the following day. In fact it was my daily routine unless I received an invite to coffee with Aella or market day and tea with Nico. So there I stood at the water's edge enjoying the simplicity of my surroundings, breathing in the freshness of the sea air, when the sound of a car disturbed me. George again, he couldn't have had another puncture surely.

'I guessed I might find you down here,' he said. How perceptive of him, we hardly knew each other. George was wearing knee length green cargo shorts and a white t-shirt, a complete contrast to how I had seen him before and he carried a large basket as he approached which looked intriguing.

'Yes, tends to be a ritual of mine,' I replied.

George pointed to the basket. 'I hope you don't mind, I have brought some brunch for us to share.'

I was speechless, my eyes wide with surprise. He couldn't have missed my reaction. I wasn't expecting another visit from him so soon and certainly not food.

'We didn't get chance to talk at the party. May I?'

'Why not,' I replied and smiled.

He lay a striped blue and white blanket out on the coarse sand, close to a few trees to give us adequate shelter from the baking sun. I sat on the blanket after the initial shock. I definitely wasn't going to turn away a free meal, even if I wasn't particularly hungry.

George proceeded to take off his shoes and then his socks. I watched him as he carefully placed a sock inside each trainer shoe. Well I guess his feet were too hot in them. And there we settled, quite idyllic, looking out as the golden sun enhanced the gentle rippling of the waves.

George unveiled the basket to reveal Eptazimo

bread, cheese and olives. The bread an island favourite, is apparently kneaded seven times (I had no idea if this was more or less than normal bread) and contains ouzo and anise, George informed me. I forced myself to eat a couple of olives but I have never been a fan to be honest, even though they are an important part of Greek cuisine. George had brought proper drinking glasses too. We drank something that had a hint of lemon, non-alcoholic, it tasted very refreshing.

I learnt that George relocated to Kalymnos following a career in the military. He had an air of self-assuredness, his fair haired head held high on top of his broad shoulders, not in an arrogant way but with confidence. George looked like he kept himself in shape and I concluded he must run most days to maintain his physique. I was interested to know if he had passed by my house before but didn't pluck up the courage to ask.

George didn't tell me what his rank had been in the military but I guessed he had risen to the position of an officer. He told me he moved to the island for a fresh start, however didn't elaborate which left me wondering. There was no mention of a partner or wife while we talked, although he did tell me he had a daughter called Millie. With a sense of pride he informed me she had graduated from Bath University and hopeful she would visit soon.

'What's your story?' George eventually asked. I guess it did appear an unusual place to settle for a woman on her own.

'Nothing very exciting,' I replied shrugging my shoulders.

George cocked his head to the right. 'Oh.' He seemed surprised by my response.

I had nothing to hide so I told him. 'My husband died and I decided to come and live here to write.' No point sugar coating my situation. I wondered if he already knew my circumstances. Had he asked Stavros about me? Was Stavros aware George sat brunching beside me? I tried not to overthink the situation and to enjoy the unexpected occasion.

'I'm sorry to hear that,' George said, his eye contact strong.

I looked up at the sky and a plane had made its mark, a stream of white scorched into the blue canvas. I resisted the urge to wave at the plane, something I often did when by myself.

'How lucky are we to be living here on Kalymnos, it's raining in England.' I lightened the mood, for his sake more than mine.

'We certainly are. And I have found a fellow Brit to keep me company. Cheers.' George raised his glass and smiled, not flirtatiously but more in a way of recognition of what I had told him.

'Cheers.' I gave a quick smile back, taking a sip, then tipping the brim of my hat forward conscious my cheeks were beginning to flush.

Sensing our conversation had stalled, neither of us appearing to have anything else to say, I seized the moment and told George I needed to get back and carry on writing. I assumed he had other things to do too. I helped him pack away and we made our way up to his car and I thought about what to say next.

George placed the picnic basket onto the cream leather seat in the back seat of his cherry red car. I had no idea of the make, it looked like a sports car, its black roof folded neatly back.

'Thank you George that was an unexpected treat.' Pleased I'd convincingly sounded grateful for the food he'd prepared for us. I couldn't remember anyone ever doing that for me.

He turned to face me and leaned against the car. 'It was my pleasure.'

I took in a breath and out came 'bye then.'

I walked away without giving him chance to reply and regretted my action, not knowing when I would meet George again.

Chapter 6

Days appeared to float by with ease, without anything to stop me writing. I had all the time in the world, no other pressures occurring stopping me achieving.

One morning as I mapped out a particular scene, my kitchen table littered with different coloured post-it notes: yellow, pink and green, when a firm knock came at the door. I wasn't expecting a visitor. Annoyed by the interruption I moved to the door to open it.

To my surprise there I found Nico, his back turned away from me studying something out at sea. I ran my fingers over my hair before he had chance to turn and face me.

'There will be a wedding tomorrow, you should come,' he said, not even a hello.

'I'm not invited,' I quickly pointed out. You

wouldn't just turn up at a wedding in England without an invite.

'You don't need an invite. Everyone is invited,' he declared with an authority I didn't dare question.

'Who are they?' I asked clinging to my open door.

'A young couple.' It would appear that was all I needed to know.

'And what about afterwards?'

'There will be a party of course.'

'Are you invited to the party?'

'Yes, but I don't usually go.' Disappointed with his reply, hoping Nico would make an exception and ask me to go to the party. Obviously we couldn't turn up together. I wondered if Aella were going, assuming she mixed with the lower classes, probably far too busy anyway.

I wasn't sure if it was something I'd seen in a film, nevertheless I asked my next question anyway. 'Will there be plate smashing?'

'Plate smashing.' Nico raised his eyebrows a fraction.

What was that film? I pondered for seconds, but nothing sprang to mind.

'I might come,' I replied. We both knew I

would.

'I must go now, I have a lot to prepare,' he said, nodding his head forward to confirm his point.

After Nico left, I considered what I should wear to a Greek wedding, although I had no intention of entering the church. I realised I needed to start investing in more clothes for different occasions should they arise. I registered it didn't really matter, after all nobody knew me.

I searched for "Smashing Plates at Greek Weddings" and apparently this custom is no longer very common. I felt an idiot.

I wore a white cotton dress and left my hair down, after I had tried a low pony tail followed by a high pony tail. I applied a light touch of lipstick to finish. I didn't want to stand out in the Greek crowd but who was I kidding. As I glanced at the image looking back at me, I saw a feminine woman and I liked what I saw. I always thought I didn't suit dresses but maybe mistaken.

Turning to leave the room I remembered another item. I opened the drawer of my dressing table and lifted out the small box, covered in different shaped shells. I slipped the silver ring on the middle finger of my right hand and let out a small sigh. It hadn't been out of the box for years and this a perfect time.

On my way to the church I was intrigued to see how this wedding would differ to English tradition. What did people wear? Did they throw anything at the bride and groom as they exited the church? I should have checked while I was looking up "plate smashing". My thoughts moved on to Nico, such an important role to play. I doubted he would even know I was there, but I just knew he would want to discuss the occasion and I wanted to be prepared with questions for him when we next met.

She wore a light fitting, strapless white gown. In her hand a posy of pure white flowers. He in his black suit and dicky bow. Their faces full of joy and love for each other, stepping out into their wedded life together. A wash of sadness flowed through me, knowing what they would share. I composed myself as tears started to well and I focused on their smiling faces.

Nico appeared at the door in a white and gold cape which dropped down at the front in two neat lines. His tall frame followed the happy couple out, now joined as man and wife. His black hair shone in the brilliant sun light. As I scanned around I was surprised by the number of people who had turned up, there must have been around fifty, not to mention how many spilled out of the small church. Did Nico get nervous, performing in front of so many?

Standing alone, most likely the only non-Greek person attending, I hoped Nico might by chance look my way and give me a reassuring smile. But if he did I may have missed it, as I took in the many smiling faces and cheering voices. I contemplated waiting until everyone had left the scene to invite Nico back for tea. Then he could tell me all about the occasion, especially what happened in the church. I changed my mind, slipping away quietly and walked in the opposite direction to the party attendees, the buzz of their voices fading as we parted further. Thankful I had witnessed the joyous occasion and maybe next time I might feel comfortable attending the celebrations that follow. If I was invited of course.

Later that afternoon I splashed sun cream on my sun kissed arms and legs and grabbed my sunhat. I poured a glass of wine and headed out into the garden, the late afternoon rays now less intense. My first sip resembling nectar, slipping down with ease. I wasn't in the habit of afternoon drinking, the beauty of living on my own meant I could do what I liked and when I liked. And after all, it was a day to celebrate.

As I sat, I rolled up the end of my dress allowing my knees and thighs to drench in sun rays. I took my second sip and let out a sigh.

'Here you are, I knocked on the door.' He startled me. Without letting go of the wine in my right hand I quickly smoothed my dress to below my knees.

'Nico.' He no longer wore the majestic cape, now in his usual attire.

Nico remained standing and looked down on me. 'I saw you there.'

'You did, I am surprised there were so many people.'

'That is a pretty dress Kate.' It was the first time Nico paid me a compliment and he caught me off guard.

My reply stupid. 'I liked your cape.'

I still had the glass in my hand and felt a sense of guilt. What must he have thought of me? It wasn't a small measure either. I placed the wine on the table.

'Please sit down Nico, I will make us tea.'

I returned inside and filled the kettle, realising I had left my wine behind. I stepped back outside, gave Nico a quick smile and grabbed the glass. I tipped my wine down the sink as the water came to boil. Then regretted my action, wondering why on earth I didn't put the wine aside for later.

'Here we are,' I announced, placing Nico's tea in front of him and we chatted about the wedding. His compliment about my dress occasionally floating to the forefront of my mind.

Chapter 7

A few weeks passed and no chance meetings with George. It crossed my mind on more than one occasion that he may stop by, my perception leading me to believe we got on quite well. Perhaps I had said something to offend or bore him? Maybe he found me too reserved? Or could it be he had other female friends to entertain in his busy diary?

I sat drinking coffee with Aella in the town and she was telling me in some detail about an expensive dress she had bought recently. I couldn't contemplate spending that amount of money on a dress.

'We should go clothes shopping together,' she said.

'Maybe.' Unsure if my budget could stretch to the extravagant tastes Aella had, then again it would be a day out and no doubt include a delicious meal so I could be persuaded.

'Aella, how well do you know George?'

'Hello,' she said, her face lighting up.

I was taken aback when George pulled up a chair, his formal dress suggesting he'd been to a meeting. He removed his sun glasses placing them into his shirt pocket and flashed Aella a smile and then the same to me. I smiled back at him and averted my gaze back to Aella. Had he heard me say his name?

Aella was on a mission to impart information to George, allowing me to conceal my embarrassment. I sat back and noticed a shared energy between Aella and George while they playfully teased one another, and if I hadn't known that Aella was married I would have guessed they were a couple, or maybe having an affair. I felt like a spectator until Aella included me.

'I'm glad you two have met, it's time Kate has some male friends,' Aella declared. I did of course have Nico, however I hadn't told Aella about him because I wasn't sure what she would make of our friendship.

I became aware of a warmness flushing my cheeks, she made me sound like a desperate singleton and I reached for my glass filled with water. I hadn't told Aella about the brunch I shared with George, although I was planning on dropping the news into our conversation during coffee. I concluded George had not disclosed this to Aella either. It was our secret it appeared.

'You should both come for dinner this Friday,' she suddenly announced.

George replied first. 'Sounds good to me, how about you Kate?' George lifted his cup whilst holding his eyes on me.

'Yes, look forward to it.' I gave them both a smile. I was looking forward to it, because the more time I spent in George's company the more he grew on me.

'Great, I'll pick you up at 7pm.'

'Okay,' I replied.

'Where do you live?' George asked.

I stared directly into his eyes and gave him directions, both knowing full well he knew where I lived. I found it hard to keep eye contact with him for too long. I spoke with composure acting out this scene for the benefit of Aella.

Aella smiled as she lifted the cup to her perfectly formed mouth. She didn't think I had seen the satisfaction shown on her face but I guessed what she was up to.

Friday arrived, and when I thought about it I was

going on a sort of date. I hadn't anticipated dating again, although I shouldn't have ruled it out, after all I was unattached and still only in my early forties.

I examined my wardrobe and didn't think I had a lot to offer the occasion. I couldn't wear the same dress I wore when I met George the first time, although I doubted he would remember. I settled on casual white linen trousers and a pale green blouse with small blue flowers, instead of flat shoes I chose a pair with a wedged heel. My hair normally tied back left down. As I sat before my dressing table mirror, I attempted to tame my curly locks as best I could using oil from the rose coloured bottle. I brought it with me to the island and figured it wasn't out of date. Although, it was purchased a number of years ago, recommended by my hairdresser for unruly hair.

My makeup routine didn't take long, mascara and lipstick my trusted friends. I made the effort to put a squirt of perfume on too, though wasn't sure how old that was either. I raised the back of my wrist to my nose and found the floral scent still smelt vibrant.

Right on time George showed up, the car engine purring. I wouldn't have expected anything less, he presented as the punctual type.

'Ready,' I said aloud to the image in front of me.

As I walked down the stairs he knocked firmly. I took in a couple of breaths and opened the door. George stood wearing black trousers and a long sleeved light blue shirt, very smart indeed. I assessed I was underdressed in comparison. In his hand, he held flowers. These I did recognise as red carnations.

'For you,' he said.

I flashed a smile. 'Thank you.'

George placed his hands into his pockets.

'Come inside while I put them in water.'

I turned on the tap, filling the vase Aella bought for me. Looking around, I spotted an unwashed plate and wished I'd made more of an effort to tidy up. Tidiness not one of my strongest qualities.

'Nice place you have here,' George said. I'm sure he was being polite and hadn't noticed the paint peeling off the walls.

'All done,' I announced, flashing a quick look at Paul's ashes. I placed the vase on my kitchen table.

George eased his car into gear and we drove off. The oil I carefully teased on earlier probably wasted as I suspected the drive was going to play havoc with my hair. I avoided the temptation to anchor it down.

I was surprised how edgy my body felt after the conversation and meal we'd already shared, well more of a picnic. I wondered if George felt nervous too and whether he classed our invite as a proper date or just an invitation to dinner with friends. Which technically it was. I didn't start the conversation and relieved when George spoke first.

'How was your day?'

How did I reply without my day sounding boring? 'Good. Yours?'

'Busy.'

Did I ask busy doing what? I didn't respond and left wondering if he thought I was hard work with my lack of conversation.

As we drove further inland and higher up, the wildlife seemed more at ease as flowers grew wildly amongst large rocks and trees. Another beautiful night and perhaps no need to fill it with pointless chat. I looked forward to the evening ahead.

We passed only a couple of properties set back from the road until we arrived at our destination. George jumped out of his car quickly and appeared at my side before I could open the door. Our hosts sat eagerly waiting for us on their terrace, bathing in the stunning view. Elvis's recognisable voice played as we climbed the steps, a favourite of Stavros. He was not however a favourite of Aella's but she tolerated the music to use to her advantage no doubt.

'A fan of Elvis are you?' George whispered in my

ear, his mouth lightly brushing my hair. I didn't respond, however couldn't contain the smirk on my face.

Aella and Stavros's marriage appeared to work like cogs in a fine working machine. I imagined my marriage would have been similar as Paul and I grew older and wiser. I wondered if George had the same thoughts when he saw Aella and Stavros together. I still had no idea of George's past, just because he had a daughter didn't mean he was once married. If I managed to speak to Aella on her own I would ask her what she knew.

Stavros poured wine from the bottle already opened and we took our seats beside him, while Aella disappeared to check on our meal. The smell wafting from Aella's cooking began to make my mouth water. Of the meals I have sampled, I can say with confidence that Aella is a wonderful cook and Stavros a great host. I was thankful for their invites and their friendship, they had taken me under their wings that I can confirm. I was quite happy living on my own, however if I hadn't met my new friends I am convinced I would have grown lonely eventually. You may have made an assumption I had run away from my old life and to a degree you are correct. However, the life of a hermit was not what I wanted at all.

A delicious smell filled the room, Aella returned with our meal of Lamb Kleftiko accompanied with a simple salad. I had missed a chance to ask her about George.

Our evening fell into a natural banter about everything and anything it appeared. George enlightened us to stories from his military days and had us all laughing as he acted out a scene. I relaxed into my chair taking in the setting, listening to my new friends.

I noticed my glass was empty. Stavros had too, he refilled my glass and left the room. Within seconds, Aella followed him.

'Having a good time?' George asked.

'Yes I am.'

'What do you expect those two are up to?' I shrugged my shoulders in response. George didn't have anything else to say as he scanned the room.

Stavros returned along with a small wooden box. He opened the lid and passed it to George. Aella also returned.

'Cuban,' Stavros said with pride.

George took a cigar out of the box and lifted it to his nose.

'The very best,' George said as he looked up at Stavros.

Stavros returned to his seat and placed the box on the table beside him. I watched Stavros with interest as he placed one of the cigars in a small metal cutter and clipped off the end with a quick strong motion. He put the cigar to his lips and did a practice draw. George passed his cigar back to Stavros and he repeated the cutting process. Stavros lit a match to create the orange flame and they both lit their cigars simultaneously, as if a great achievement had been made. It appeared an intimate moment shared between two men. I'd never sampled a cigar and wished I had been brave enough to ask.

Stavros relaxed into his chair, a puff of smoke leaving his lips, he turned his attention on me. 'Kate.'

'Yes Stavros.'

'Tell me, how is your book coming along?'

'It is developing quite nicely,' I replied cautiously, expecting it would not be left at that.

'And the main character, what is his name?' I couldn't remember telling Stavros the main character was a man, yet it was possible and therefore didn't challenge his male chauvinism.

'Thomas.'

'Not Stavros?' Stavros tapped the arm of his chair with his free hand gently but with purpose.

'No, not for this story.' I smiled at Stavros.

'George is a strong name and has more history.' George allowed a smirk to grace his face and then placed the cigar to his lips.

Stavros pointed his finger in George's direction. 'In your country maybe.'

'Your next book should have a heroine, you can use my name Kate,' Aella chipped in.

'Valid point Aella,' George said firmly and a tactful move.

'So you will be writing more stories?' Stavros quickly added, his posture relaxed not tempted to take on his worthy male opponent.

'I hope to Stavros,' I replied.

'Perhaps I can help you?' Stavros winked at me. Stavros was persistent and I suspected a frustrated writer may be hidden within him. An idea popped up, maybe he could read my first draft and give me his views.

After coffee we departed, it was around 11.30pm, not too early to be unsociable but late enough to call it a night.

'Enjoy your drive home,' Aella whispered in my ear as we hugged our farewell.

George was quiet on the way back. I made up for this as I'd had quite a few glasses of wine compared to his couple. I can't recall what I was talking about. When I glanced at George he appeared more interested in the road ahead of us, which I thought rude at the time. And then we quickly arrived at my place.

George switched off the engine and I stayed seated not knowing whether to stay put or get out. My nerves getting the better of me, as I tried to figure out whether to speak or depart and relieved when he broke the quietness first.

'That was an excellent evening, great food and company.'

I turned my head to face him and his fingers still clung to the steering wheel. I hadn't quite worked George out, one minute he appeared extremely confident taking charge of conversations, laughing and joking and then he appeared shy. Not shy, reserved more fitting.

'Yes it was.'

The wine I drank earlier suddenly lost its affect and I couldn't think of anything else to say. George stared ahead, I wasn't sure if he was disappointed by my brief reply or if he searched for what to say next. I waited letting an uncomfortable silence surround us, the islands creatures retired for the night.

Time to make my move and I opened my mouth to speak. George beat me to it.

'Can I see you again?' George asked.

'Yes,' I fired back surprising myself. His hands relaxed from their grip on the steering wheel and he placed them onto his muscular thighs.

'How about next Monday?'

I delayed my answer as I registered Monday would be tricky; being market day and Nico would join me for tea and chat.

'Could we make it Tuesday instead?' I answered, implying I had a busy social life, which was far from the truth. To be honest I was astonished George wanted to see me again so soon.

'Tuesday it is,' he replied. Satisfied with my response or maybe just as nervous as me, George stepped out of his car. I didn't make my move, expecting he would want to open my door. It seemed an old fashioned thing to do.

'I'll pick you up at 10,' George stated.

As I stood behind the closed door, squeezing my shoulders into a hug, I took in a deep breath and let a smile fill my face.

The engine roared as George drove away.

Chapter 8

Tuesday came around quickly. I'd been to the market the previous day but no Nico, even though I stayed a little longer prolonging my visit and it concerned me that he wasn't there. I considered checking in at the church and then talked myself out of it. Was he unwell? I had no way of checking, I didn't know where he lived. Come to think of it where did he live? Perhaps in accommodation attached to the church. I doubted that would be the case. I made a mental note to ask him the next time I saw him.

I sat at my kitchen table and a firm knock alerted me to George's arrival. I took in a deep breath and exhaled as I made my way to open the door. He stood before me wearing his knee length cargo shorts again and a navy t-shirt, casual George again. However this time he wore a blue helmet on his head, in his hand he held another one.

George pointed to my hat. 'You won't be needing that today.'

'Clearly not.'

He stayed put while I locked the door and then I slipped the key into my pocket. George walked towards a black moped parked at the side of my house and I followed.

He turned to me. 'Our transport, it's the best way to travel on the island.' I didn't feel qualified to respond and gave him a smile instead.

Excited to get going, I stepped closer to the moped ready to straddle the seat, thankful I had chosen to wear shorts for our outing. George turned to face me and sensing my eagerness placed his free hand firmly on top of my shoulder. He gently placed the other helmet on my head and fastened the strap with precision.

'Now you can jump on board.' His eyes locked purposely.

As I seated, I was hit with a sudden flash back to when we had gone on our moped trip to Pothia. Remembering what we both wore, the taste of the ice cream, getting lost on the way back. The images crystal clear, as if it happened yesterday. To know I could never share that day, or any day together again still stabbed at my heart, and then to be sharing this experience with George. That such a special memory could be replaced with another.

'Hold on tight,' George said, blocking my

thoughts of grief.

George sped off quickly, keen to get going. How tight I initially considered, placing my hands around his waist. As George increased our speed my grip got stronger, I had no choice I didn't want to fall off! Although, fairly confident George wasn't a novice.

A wave of excitement hit me, a tingling sensation flooding my body. My senses heightened to find George surprisingly toned for a man in his late forties. Not that I had any experience of wrapping my arms around men of late. In fact I didn't know George's actual age and thought I would be able to casually slip in the question during the day. It occurred to me that there was so much more we didn't know about each other.

We took the coastal route with its meandering roads, the sea in constant view. A slight brush of breeze kissed my skin as the road took us higher. I hadn't appreciated the coastline from this perspective and how the power of the water had continually eroded the land, defining its shape over time. My mind absorbing the view, yet still conscious of his body radiating into my arms and hands. I wondered what George was thinking about and how aware he was of my touch.

Our journey appeared seamless encountering no other forms of transport as if we had hired the road to ourselves for the day. And then just as I thought we couldn't go much higher, George stopped.

'Okay?' George asked.

'Yes all good,' I replied.

George slowed his speed and we began the steep decline, winding our way down. At the bottom we arrived at a small harbour filled with a few local fishing boats, back from their morning search. Kalymnos is also known as Sponge Divers Island. I'd never met a diver before and wondered if it were a dangerous occupation and if exceptional lung capacity was a prerequisite. I guess unless I spoke to a diver I'd never find out. Maybe this was my chance. Aella gave me one of the natural sponges, wrapped in tissue paper and told me it would be far better for my skin. A strange gift I thought at the time, however it looked like it worked for her and I accepted the sponge gracefully hoping it would have the same effect on me. To be honest I haven't noticed much difference, then again I only use the sponge when I remember.

George parked the moped outside one of the tavernas and we were immediately greeted by a waiter, keen for customers as if his first of the day. We followed him in and he placed us at a table looking out across the harbour, its bobbing boats now empty of their crews.

Our waiter quickly returned and handed us each a menu. George announced he had been here once before and the food tasted delicious, so on that basis I let him order for me. A brief thought came to mind, maybe I wasn't the first female he had brought here on his moped, but I had no way of proving it. Although why did he have two helmets?

Two bottles of beer arrived at our table. George took his first sip and then let out a contented sigh. I mirrored his actions, feeling at ease in my new surroundings.

'Do you miss being in the military George?'

He smiled in response to my question. 'I do. Especially in my early career.' George paused as if recalling a time in his mind, his fingers on his left hand playfully massaging the fair hair on his head. I waited for him to enlighten me.

'My first overseas posting was in Cyprus. I couldn't believe my luck, the weather glorious just like here. I was in my early twenties, confident and naive about life. One of the chaps, Jimmy, decided to help himself to a truck one night and about ten of us piled in. Jimmy took us into the nearby town. The plan, hmm, was to have a couple of drinks and get back to the base without anyone noticing we'd left. One drink led to several as we played a game called killer pool. Ever played that?'

'Can't say I have,' I replied.

George continued. 'Each player has three lives, and you take a single shot to pot a ball. If you fail, you lose a life and take a drink, simple game.' George took a drink of his beer. 'A couple of the lads, now what were their names?' George asked of himself. 'One was big John, and the other lucky Luke, we just called him Lucky. Both pretty decent pool players when sober. Anyway there were some locals in the bar that night while we played the game. Lucky could see them staring our way and challenged them. There was no doubt in our minds our lads couldn't lose as we cheered them on rowdily. But they did lose.' George took another drink of his beer.

'What happened next?' I asked.

'It got messy, a few punches were thrown, maybe some broken noses, definitely bloody noses. I remember stepping in beside the owner to try and calm our lads down. Not surprisingly, we were told to leave. We all piled back into the truck with Jimmy behind the wheel, full of booze and he drove us to a nearby beach. Someone thought it would be a good idea to jump off a cliff. God only knows how one of us didn't drown.'

Our dish arrived, steam rising from the prawns and feta cheese in its rich tomato and vegetable sauce, accompanied by bread of course. A strong smell of garlic wafting into the air, I couldn't wait to try the dish it smelt and looked amazing. My taste buds were not disappointed, first sweet then spicy flavours enlightened my palate.

'This is delicious George.'

'Don't waste any,' he said.

I looked down to locate where I had spilt my food and couldn't spot anything. George lent forward and I froze. His hand rose and with his crisp white napkin he gently wiped whatever was on my chin. I smiled awkwardly and thankfully the waiter appeared with a second beer.

I grabbed for my bottle and took a sip.

'So what about you. You haven't always been a writer,' he quizzed. I didn't want to bore him with the ins and outs of profit and loss.

'I was good with figures.'

George raised his eyebrows. 'Anything else?'

'Maybe.'

'That's not playing fair.' When I didn't respond George carried on eating his meal.

Almost immediately after we had both finished eating our waiter appeared with the bill. I reached for my purse and George lifted his hand insisting on paying, even though I was quite prepared to pay my share. I didn't make an issue of it and reasoned I could treat him the next time, assuming there would be one.

I was feeling a contented fullness from our meal as we strolled leisurely around the harbour.

We came across a couple of shops and we took our time to browse around, one of which sold painted headscarves, another industry from the island. I picked up a scarf, turning it over in my hands, George suggested I try it on.

The lady owner led me to a long mirror and showed me how to tie the scarf correctly. I glanced at George, he leaned against a nearby wall watching on with interest, while I took a couple of attempts to master the simple task.

'That colour matches your eyes,' he said. Was he flirting with me?

'And what colour are they?' I didn't look his way.

Amused by our banter, the owner's mouth formed a smile.

'Blue of course. And grey.' I was impressed, my left eye blue, my right more of a grey.

I removed the scarf and placed it back to its original place and smiled apologetically at the owner as I made my way out of her shop, assuming George followed. He appeared soon after and placed a small paper bag into my hand. George didn't say anything as I peeped inside to find he had bought the scarf for me. I looked up and the corners of his mouth formed a subtle smile. His eye contact held firm.

'Thank you.' I started walking trying to contain the smug grin upon my face.

This is going well I thought as we made our way back to the moped. George hadn't mentioned going anywhere else, therefore I assumed we were heading back. I suppose I shouldn't have expected he had a whole day free to spend with me, but I didn't want it to end just yet.

On our way back I quite happily held on to George again, climbing the winding road, fully aware of how close our bodies touched. I wondered what George sensed from our closeness.

We had only been on the bike for a short time when George veered over to the side of the road and came to a gradual stop. Had we run out of petrol or a puncture crossed my mind.

'Okay if we stop by my place?' he asked.

Naturally I replied yes, curious to see where he lived, his life appeared a mystery to me.

Chapter 9

When we arrived I was quite taken aback. His house sat back from the road and much bigger than mine, in fact it resembled a mansion in comparison. George switched off the engine.

'You can jump off first,' he said removing his helmet.

He opened the tall ornate gate and I followed him as he pushed the bike up a paved path. Half way along we came across a man at work engrossed in his sweeping. George nodded to him as we passed.

'Come, I'll show you around,' George said. I have to say I was extremely intrigued as we entered through a rich mahogany door to George's castle.

The inside of the house appeared immaculate as we walked straight into a living room upon a grey and white marble effect floor. It could have been the real thing it looked authentic. The room was sparse of furniture but understandable since he hadn't been on the island long or maybe that was his preferred taste. What furniture he did have appeared expensive and put my second hand purchases to shame. Not forgetting a grand piano, the shiny dark wood showing the beauty of its grain. I wondered if George played.

George didn't appear to want to linger and I followed him through an arch into a hall. A staircase spiralled before us and as I looked up a large chandelier took centre stage. Before I knew it we were heading to the back of the house and into daylight once again.

To say I was shocked an understatement at what transpired before me; rows upon rows of trees lined up like soldiers. George didn't have a garden, he had a vineyard! I quickly closed my gaping mouth before George turned his gaze my way.

'George, this is impressive.'

'I wanted to show you what I actually do for a living.'

I stood and marvelled at the magnificent sight.

'Shall we.' George signalled the way.

I followed George down stone steps towards the vineyard and we walked side by side along a dusty track, wide enough for a narrow cart perhaps? No sign of any workers and the only audible sound a gentle rustling of leaves.

George stopped and stepped between the rows of trees. Not knowing if he wanted me to wait I trusted my instincts and followed him in.

'Try this one.' George turned to face me and placed a shiny red grape into my hand.

The first thing I noticed, it appeared smaller than the ones you get to eat and when I placed it into my mouth the skin appeared rougher. I bit down and realised the mistake, my mouth filling with seeds. I tried to conceal my stupidity of putting the whole grape into my mouth and reluctantly swallowed while George watched me. And then he smiled without pointing out the obvious.

He picked several more as we entered in further, inspecting each one before trying their taste. George seemed keen to tell me about his passion by way of bold gestures and an excitable energy until he came to an abrupt stop.

'Sorry, I get carried away.'

'Its fine George, don't stop. It's not every day I get to visit a vineyard.' I smiled to reassure him and he smiled back. An unspoken tension between us for a brief moment and then he stepped towards me, his hand reaching forward to the side of my face, his fingers gently tucking back a strand of wayward hair.

He turned first and led us back, a silence wedged between us. My brain trying to make sense of the intimate moment shared.

We approached the rear of his house, George paused and pointed to another building a few yards from the main house. 'The next part of your tour.'

George pulled open the large heavy door. Inside we found wooden barrels overflowing with grapes as George told me what would happen to them next with great expertise. I noticed a few crates of wine stacked against one wall, ready to be sold I assumed. George followed my gaze.

'Here take one.' He handed a bottle over to me. A gold coloured label read something in Greek I couldn't translate, although that was not an issue because it was red, my favourite.

'Thank you George.' One kind gesture after another with this man and he seemed genuine. How could he be single? He appeared to be ticking all the right boxes.

'Right, best get you back to your place,' he announced.

This time we travelled in George's sports car. On our way back, the sun had begun to retire for the night, the sky picture perfect displaying shades of orange tinged with pink. An artist's dream.

George slowly brought his car to a standstill and switched off the engine. He turned his body to face mine and rested his arm around the back of my seat.

'Thanks for a great day,' I quickly said.

'You're welcome,' George replied the corners of his mouth forming a smile. Was he aware how good looking he was?

'Next time, you can choose our adventure.' He winked cheekily.

He caught me off guard, unsure I could top our day out together, but that doubt quickly replaced with an uncontrollable smirk. George wanted to see me again.

'I'll think of something.' A fluttery sensation developed inside as I answered George and his arm had not moved. A sudden shyness got the better of me. 'Good night George.'

Closing my door I remembered I'd forgotten to ask him his age but then again he hadn't asked me mine. Really, that was my lasting thought. Frustrated I could be so shallow after a fantastic day, I tutted to myself.

I placed the wine on the table next to his flowers, still alive.

I sent a short message. "You didn't tell me he owned a vineyard!! Speak soon x"

Chapter 10

Just gone four on a Sunday afternoon, almost a week after my day out with George on the moped, when I decided to try on the headscarf. I sat in front of my dressing room mirror, tying the scarf securely remembering how the lady had shown me. What had she made of us two? Probably assumed George was my husband and he bought the special gift for his wife.

Surprisingly it took just the one attempt and I admired my handy work. Definitely a look I hadn't tried out before and a smirk appeared as I recalled our day out together. I never imagined I would meet someone like George on the island, he was bringing out a hidden sense of adventure in me and I was looking forward to more.

Since I'd moved to the island I had become lazy, I didn't have an excuse. In the past I'd never been a gym goer, there didn't seem a need and I wasn't too fussed about exercise in general. I guess I've been blessed in that my metabolism keeps me relatively slim. Although we did head out most weekends in the warmer months on our bikes, even with me lagging behind Paul. Our reward, stopping for a well-earned pint and a bite to eat at one of our favourite watering holes. After Paul died I didn't venture out on my bike again. I gave both bikes away to my next door neighbours' kids.

The thought of enquiring if I could buy a bike reached the surface of my mind, would have to be robust, the roads not great where I lived. Perhaps George had one of those too or at least knew where to buy one.

On my way downstairs I remembered I needed to water my plants, determined not to let them die. Although I couldn't promise anything. I grabbed a large jug and filled it with water and headed into the garden.

The plants soaked up the water with such thirst and I found a sudden sense of pride at the sight of my flowers flourishing. I was looking forward to Nico's next visit to gain his approval. Although his recent absence at the market still niggled a little as to why he wasn't there. Still, I reasoned perhaps he might bring me more plants now that I had passed the test, which would mean investing in more pots from somewhere.

I considered if I should get Nico something in return. What did one buy for a priest? I didn't even know the month of his birthday and he none the wiser of mine. I suspected he was a Libran, the sign depicted as scales. He seemed well balanced. As I pondered, my thoughts were interrupted by the sound of a car engine followed by men's voices. I wasn't expecting anyone and made my way gingerly around to the front of the house.

Totally out of the blue Jack stood there, earphones in, singing away, about to knock on my door. Flabbergasted to see him an understatement as he stood in ripped jeans and a dark blue t-shirt. At his feet lay an oversized holdall. I hadn't clapped eyes on my brother or spoken to him for that matter since I left England. I'd sent him a postcard a month after arriving and I received the one text "Looks nice".

Jack resembled a surfer dude with his blonde wavy hair, devilishly handsome and very much aware of this judging by the confident smile on his face. The pleasant sight before me a far cry from his acne filled face as a teenager.

I marched towards him, one hand on my hip the other still holding the jug. 'Jack, wow. Why didn't you call me?'

'I thought I'd surprise you,' he said and proceeded to lift me up in a bear hug almost squeezing the life out of me.

'Let me down. I can't believe you are here.' He let me go and looked down on me.

'Nice scarf, is that what all the women are wearing here?'

I pulled the scarf off my head and opened the unlocked door. My brother followed me inside.

Turned out Jack had been made redundant from his highly paid PR job based in London. When he first notified me of the job a couple of years previously I expected he would be a good fit for it, he oozed confidence, never one to doubt his abilities. However, something had changed and this job clearly wasn't for him anymore. He told me he resigned to the fact he was going to leave anyway because he was getting bored of the place and people. Then luckily for him the chance to volunteer for redundancy presented itself. I had no reason to doubt his motives, it sounded plausible enough. To my knowledge, Jack didn't stay in any job too long and if he didn't like something, he didn't hang around. I admired that quality, he wasn't a people pleaser he did what was right for him. He also informed me he was in between girlfriends and to be honest I couldn't keep up with his love life either. Despite the fact Jack approached his mid-thirties it appeared he had no intention of settling down.

After the initial shock of his arrival I was genuinely pleased to see him and realised I should have invited him sooner. Perhaps he assumed I had become a recluse and got sick of waiting for an invite. In the back of my mind, I doubted his arrival was because he worried for my welfare, more like he wanted a free holiday.

I rustled up some food and provided beer from my limited stock and we settled in the garden. And quite quickly laughter and reminiscing about days growing up came to light. We spoke of friends we once knew and speculated where they were now.

Jack took a swig of his beer. 'What was that boy called you went out with, who lived near the park?'

'Which boy?'

'You know, the one who swore outside our house and dad went mad.' Jack had an impressive memory, I couldn't think of who he referred to. He was going back a lot of years.

'Harry. That was his name. Great footballer,' he added.

'Oh yes, Harry.' Harry was a couple of years older than me, I think I was only fourteen at that time. In my eyes we were friends not boyfriend and girlfriend. My friends would tease me because Harry used to wait for me at the school gate and walk me home. I wondered what Harry was up to now, maybe he did get to be a professional footballer. I couldn't check his surname escaped me.

After we finished our second and final beer, I cleared away the plates. Jack followed me in and rummaged around in the holdall he had discarded on the floor. He took out a bottle.

'Here you go. Don't suppose you have anything to mix with it.'

'No, I don't.'

'Oh well, we'll just have a couple of shots then. Where are your glasses?'

'In that cupboard,' I replied pointing. Thinking just the one for me.

Eventually we retired to our rooms, Jack had to settle for my spare room, the one I hadn't got around to sorting out. Thank goodness the previous owner left a single bed in it. I found some sheets and a spare pillow and tried not to worry about Jack's six foot something frame squeezed into it. With all the alcohol consumed that night, I'm sure he didn't notice.

As I lay on my bed, my head sinking back into the pillows, I let out a sigh. I was still stunned from Jack's arrival. Certainly something I needed to get used to; having him stay with me and I hoped he wouldn't judge me too harshly by what he found. I did have one further thought before I finally slept, would Jack be here long enough to be introduced to my new friends.

Little did I know that the following two weeks

after Jack's arrival were going to be eventful, very eventful indeed!

Chapter 11

Market day. I woke up a little later than usual, no doubt due to the amount of alcohol consumed the night before. Unfortunately one shot turned into a few for me, but not as many as Jack! I considered going in to wake him, but after lightly knocking on the door and hearing no answer, I resolved to leave him in bed to sleep off both his journey and his possible hangover. I then speculated it was probably best not to be seen with him at the market, just in case people surmised I had now taken up with a toy boy. Although that might have been quite amusing.

Nico stood there, talking to one of the market sellers. I hadn't seen him since his no show the previous week and still puzzled why he hadn't been there. I watched him a little longer until he turned around and spotted me. He strode over to where I stood. I tried not to make it obvious I waited for him, fiddling with my watch strap.

'Hello Nico, I was just leaving.' We both knew I was lingering.

As had become a custom he asked if he could help me with my shopping. Glancing at the time I didn't think Jack would be awake, so I kindly accepted Nico's offer.

On our walk back, I told Nico about my brother's shock arrival the previous day. Nico always the attentive listener let me waffle on, to be honest he didn't have much choice and in no time at all we arrived at my house.

All of a sudden Jack appeared at the door. He filled it to the top his head slightly bent forward.

'Oh Jack you are up and about.' I think he was a bit taken aback I had a priest in tow by his opened mouth reaction.

I looked from my brother to Nico and back to my brother again.

'This is Nico, I mean Nicolaos, he is a priest at the local church,' I announced. Undoubtedly he was a priest what a stupid thing to say, he certainly wasn't on his way to a fancy dress party. Anyhow if he were, he would have definitely won.

Jack played it cool, a slight nod of his head. His

silence embarrassing. Nico stayed rooted to the spot.

'Would you like to stay for tea Nicolaos?' I filled the space, now conscious of how small I appeared between two giants.

'I'll make it,' Jack said, in a rush to leave the scene not giving Nico chance to answer.

Using my assertive voice. 'No, you sit with Nicolaos in the garden, I'll make it.'

I disappeared inside abandoning my shopping bags, an orange escaping across the floor. I registered my insistence was too impulsive, Jack and Nico had nothing in common. I suspected Jack wouldn't be comfortable talking to a priest. Although, I guessed he had plenty he could confess given the chance. There was of course the time when Jack was in his late teens, seeing a married woman for a while (twenty years his senior), that was until her husband found out and decided to pay her secret lover a visit. Jack lived under the same roof as our parents at the time!

I made haste and returned with three teas placing them on the table. Both Jack and Nico were looking out across the landscape. An awkward silence.

'Jack was telling me about his job in London,' Nico said. His job no longer I wanted to add, but wasn't sure if Jack had omitted that on purpose or hadn't got around to telling him that part yet.

I picked up a tea and parked myself on the nearby wall, my only two chairs filled.

'What about you Nico, have you attempted any other jobs?' I didn't tell Jack to shorten Nico's name, and I wasn't sure where Jack was going with this line of question.

'Me. No.' Nico put his cup to his mouth and drank. This is going well I thought and I tried to conjure up something to say to move the conversation along.

'I've only had a couple myself,' I added, not exactly riveting conversation.

I sensed Nico wouldn't stay much longer and wasn't surprised when he stood.

'I need to be back at the church. Good to meet you Jack.' Nico turned his gaze at me, his eyes locked with mine for a couple of seconds and then the briefest of smiles and he walked away.

I cleared the cups from the table.

'Couldn't shut him up could we,' Jack said in a sarcastic tone. 'So, when did you start going to church?'

'I don't.' I returned inside, picked up the runaway orange and started to unpack the food. Jack stood watching me. I figured he was going to say or ask something about Nico.

'No wonder you like it here,' he said.

'What do you mean?' Of course I knew he was referring to Nico.

'He's a good looking man, I mean priest.' Jack stated the obvious.

'He's just a friend Jack, who helps me with my shopping.' I felt the heat in my cheeks as I busily put items into the fridge as slowly as possible, moving food around, hoping the coldness might cool me down. I realised how stupid my reply sounded.

'I wonder if he offers this service to others,' Jack muttered. 'What is there to do around here?' Jack changed the subject thank goodness.

'Not a lot really, I'm here to write,' I replied. Jack hadn't done his research, if he wanted excitement he wouldn't find it here.

'Yes, but you must get out and meet other people. Or is your only friend Nico the priest?' Jack's question mocking me.

'Don't be silly, I have other friends, just not too many and I like it this way.' Although if Jack's welcome was like that to my other friends, the few that I had, I wondered if I'd have any left.

'So, where are you taking me tonight?' I detected anticipation in his question.

I turned to face my brother crossing my arms.

'Well on the basis you just turned up out of the blue, I haven't had a lot of time to arrange a welcoming party.'

'There must be somewhere you can go for a night out, surely?' I sensed desperation in Jack's voice.

'We can go to one of the tavernas in the town.' I didn't tell him there were only three in total.

'Great, what can I eat now?' Jack asked.

I had an extra mouth to feed and would now need to buy a lot more food and drink while Jack was staying with me, he obviously hadn't grown to that size by grazing.

I threw an apple his way, whereupon he wiped it on his thigh.

'It's been washed,' I said in protest.

Jack munched noisily.

I wasn't prepared for having visitors and moved here for a reason and that included leaving the life I left behind. My old life was filled amid formality and busyness and certainly wasn't surrounded by the nature I woke up to every day. My new life had a casualness to it which suited me just fine. I had no inkling how long Jack planned to stay for, though he'd only brought a holdall, and unsure if my steady pace of life would bore him quickly. I decided to broach the subject over dinner that evening to find out his intentions.

On our walk to the taverna, the evening air felt warm on my skin. I think Jack was surprised when I told him we would be walking and I didn't have my own transport. So far I hadn't needed a car as the stroll into town took ten minutes. There are local buses delivering you to other towns and villages should the need arise. I also knew I could ask Stavros if I needed to borrow a car. I never have.

I took Jack to the taverna 'Kali Orexi' in the main square. The name translates into bon appétit and is the most pleasing to the eye out of the three with its welcoming cornflower blue sign. Jack had been working and living in London for quite some time and I presumed he ate at expensive restaurants with an abundance of choice too. I was fairly confident he would find the food tasty even if the decor and presentation wasn't up to his usual standard.

As we approached the taverna a black and white cat lay on the large step, its eyes closed shut while it blissfully slept. The owner recognised me. 'Yasou,' he said and welcomed us in with a huge grin, his shortness made even more obvious, Jack towering over him resembling a giraffe.

We were led through the dimly lit room to be seated, our table covered with a red and white checked cloth and its matching white chairs. Fairly quiet inside, the only other table occupied by two Greek men deep in conversation, shrouded in cigarette smoke, oblivious to our arrival. You have to imagine this part of the island is not a big draw for tourists, therefore is usually only frequented by locals and I liked it that way.

The owner, whose name I didn't know and should have made an effort to ask on a previous visit, handed us each a menu and proceeded to light the candle on our table. I ordered red wine and the owner moved away allowing us to make our choices.

'Anything take your fancy?' I asked Jack.

Jack's eyes were fixated on something behind my left shoulder.

'You choose,' he replied, his gaze still set.

I perused the choices before me, contemplating what Jack would enjoy. 'How about lemon chicken?' I ordered this with Aella on a previous visit and it tasted delicious.

'Great.' Jack's line of vision concentrated further and his interest had arrived.

Our waitress poured the wine slowly and Jack couldn't take his eyes off her. She was stunning, no doubt about that, her dark brown hair tumbling down her back. Jack was hooked, she gave him a scarce glance to tempt him more as she placed the bottle on our table. She turned her back away from his stare returning to her duties.

'What was that?' Jack brushed his hand down towards his calf. I glanced down and the sleeping cat had awoken and now on the look out for food.

'Just a cat.'

Jack eyeballed our new guest. 'Do they bite? I can't remember when I last had a tetanus.'

I stifled a snigger. 'Of course not, there's lots of stray cats here. Just ignore it.'

Jack glanced down again and his new friend wasn't in a rush to move.

'Scat!' he said and the cat nonchalantly moved on.

During our meal, I had an inkling we were being watched. I glanced around and he sat on his own tucked away in a corner. Somehow he had slipped into the taverna while we were engaged in conversation. Probably wondering who the handsome younger man I sat with might be, our table romantically enhanced by the flickering of the candle flame. Could he have been a wee bit jealous? I smiled and gestured him over.

'Kate, it's good to see you,' George said, not quite as formally attired dressed in a blue checked shirt and jeans.

'George this is Jack.' I chose to make him suffer a little longer and not disclose who the younger, handsome man I dined with.

'Oh, good to meet you Jack.' George shook Jack's hand and remained standing, his shoulders back as they appeared to scrutinize each other.

'Jack is my brother,' I stated. A grin emerged on George's face. 'Take a seat and join us.'

'Thank you, but no. I only popped in for a swift one, I'm eating over at Stavros's place tonight.' George drank up the last of his wine.

I was still intrigued to know how George and Stavros had met and realised I didn't use the opportunity to ask when we were both invited to dinner. Perhaps there wasn't a mystery at all and I was reading into a scenario that didn't exist.

The owner appeared holding an unusual shaped green bottle and handed it to George.

'Enjoy the rest of your evening, I'm heading off now,' George stated.

'Okay, send them my regards,' I said and watched George leave.

As soon as George departed, I knew exactly what Jack was going to say, so predictable.

'I repeat, no wonder you like it here.' He raised his eyebrows. 'Another one of your friends?'

Thankfully the dimness in the taverna hiding a slow glow of my cheeks yet again. I hated the way my face gave away my feelings.

On our walk home I thought about George and when I would meet him again. I was also thinking of the last time I saw him and regretting getting out of his car so quickly.

'That was a decent meal,' Jack said disrupting my thoughts.

Chapter 12

Jack's third day and during breakfast I decided to ask him what his plans were, as I'd failed the task the night before.

'So, how long do I have the pleasure of your company, dear brother?' Tactful I thought.

'A couple of weeks should do it, but if you think I will get in the way of your writing I could try and book into a hotel, presuming they have one?' he said shrugging his shoulders.

Two weeks didn't sound too bad, I knew I could cope with that, especially as I had progressed reasonably ahead of where I needed to be with my story, therefore it could work out nicely.

'Sure, I wouldn't dream of you staying anywhere else,' I told him.

I needed to buy more food from the town now that I had a guest staying with me and I asked Jack to join me. I suspected he was more than happy to get out of the house and investigate why I was attracted to this island. Not knowing what he'd presumed before he turned up. He may have been shocked, I never informed him the house came with a pool. And then there was the matter of the plumbing which took a little getting used to.

Shortly after arriving in the town we bumped into Aella, modelling an off the shoulder yellow sundress, highlighting her enviable tanned skin. Of course she couldn't wait to be introduced to Jack. She had heard on the grapevine my brother was visiting and I wondered who told her ..... George?

'You didn't tell me you had a handsome, younger brother Kate.'

'Didn't I?' Come to think of it Aella had never asked if I had any siblings, she didn't seem intrigued about my family and friends at all apart from my late husband.

'Let's have coffee, assuming you have time Jack?'

"Assuming you have time Jack", what about me? Jack appeared bowled over by Aella's beauty and more than happy to oblige her request.

We sat at Aella's favourite table in the shade next to a small stone fountain. A trickle of water just audible over the chatter of voices and hum of activity on another glorious day. Coffee in Greece is a serious affair and can last a long time as Aella once explained to me. Apparently it is the best way for non-Greeks to start socialising with Greek people. When I met with Aella, I often wondered how many hours a day Greeks actually worked, if they sat around drinking coffee for hours on end.

I may as well have not been there. Aella sat forward on her seat twiddling her no doubt expensive pearls, asking so many questions of Jack and he willingly replied. In fact I learnt quite a lot about my brother as he fell into a natural ease. For instance, he had broken up with his girlfriend Emma of six months because he was cheating on her with her cousin. Apparently he met the cousin at Emma's brother's wedding. He slipped out with the cousin for a crafty smoke and ended up snogging her. Since when did he start smoking? They swapped numbers and had been seeing each other secretly. He got caught out when he sent a text message meant for the cousin to Emma. Aella appeared amused by Jack's antics, laughing somewhat louder than I thought necessary.

'I didn't know you smoked?' I asked changing the mood.

'It was just a phase.'

'What else have you tried?' I realised I should have chosen my moment to ask this question just in case Jack's response was a shocker.

Jack shook his head from side to side. 'Probably best you don't know.'

Aella stared at me and tapped the tip of her nose with her index finger twice. Jack and Aella appeared to have struck up an unlikely partnership.

'You will have to come to dinner Jack, I will arrange something soon,' Aella said, not put off by my brother's antics. I presumed I was invited too and off she went leaving us to pay the bill. Jack sank back into his chair, staring hungrily at Aella's enviable figure as she walked away.

We left shortly afterwards and bought a few provisions for a light lunch and an evening meal and headed back to the house.

'Aella seems a fun person to be around and extremely attractive,' Jack said, emphasising the word extremely. As Aella didn't mention Stavros, I suspected Jack deduced he might be in with a chance. It was likely he had checked out Aella's left hand and deduced she wasn't married since Greek's wear their rings on the right. Or perhaps assumed she was a divorcee. I decided to have a bit of fun with his comment.

'Yes she is. Your type is she?'

'Definitely,' he replied, no hesitation.

'I thought you preferred blondes.'

'I've been out with loads of dark haired beauties,' he quickly pointed out. I didn't doubt that.

'Keep your eyes off Aella, she is happily married to a wealthy and important man who would eat you for breakfast.' That was the warning I gave him.

Jack didn't say another word.

After lunch, I made the decision to make Jack's room more comfortable for his stay and spurred into action to have a long overdue clear out. He said it wasn't necessary, stretching his long body out on my sofa, knocking cushions to the floor in the process, but I insisted.

I kneeled down and looked under Jack's bed. It's amazing what you find in boxes and question what possessed you to keep things for. I wasn't ruthless enough with what travelled with me, especially when I came across a silver coloured medal I received from my dancing days. I thought I'd got rid of all those, so I guess it must have meant something. Then it came to me, I was awarded the top award: a grade distinction. Maybe I should have stuck at it and not given up dancing for socialising with my friends.

My hobby was dancing and Jack's swimming. I concluded I got a better deal because I didn't have to get up at unsociable hours to train. Give Jack his due, he kept at it and became quite successful his bedroom shelves filled with cups and medals galore. I tossed the medal into the pile of things I'd decided to get rid of.

My hand found a small hard object; a wooden blue carriage on red wheels, probably part of a loved train set that had been left behind. I reached in again to pull out another box, this one containing loose photographs. As I spread them out on the floor around me I found one of me and Jack as children, only our heads visible while we lay buried in the golden Cornish sand. I remembered that day, dad helping me bury Jack first and then he buried me after. I could just make out the shape of my construction it resembled a mermaid, I had no idea what Jack's was supposed to be. I sat gazing at our innocent smiling faces, little did they know what life had install for them. I was surprised how the photo moved me, like a song that you love but can also make you cry. I let out a small sigh.

I didn't put the photo back in the box and instead left it resting on the small table next to Jack's bed. I hadn't a clue what to do with the toy and then I put it in the box along with the photos to be placed under the bed once again. I finished the room with a good clean and there was a moderate improvement. Probably needed a coat of paint if I was honest but at least it contained a little less clutter. I closed the door to my guest's room and found Jack at the foot of the stairs.

'Where have you been hiding?' he asked.

'Spring cleaning your room just as I told you. Lonely without me?' I teased.

Jack's eyebrows lifted and then he told me he wanted to take a stroll along the sea front. I gave him some pointers of where he could walk to, giving me an opportunity to carry on writing.

An hour later Jack arrived back.

'I just spotted your priest walking past the house, he saw me and carried on,' Jack announced, joining me at the kitchen table.

I looked up mid-sentence. 'Oh yes.' Clearly he wasn't my priest but I chose not to challenge Jack's statement and carried on typing.

It did seem strange that Nico hadn't stopped by and I became curious to who else he could be visiting. I would have enjoyed a catch up over tea especially as he had already been introduced to Jack. I wanted them to meet again, hoping they would get on. In my eyes who wouldn't get on with Nico?

True to form Aella invited us to dinner for the following night. Blimey she was keen, Jack had only been here for a few days. She informed me on the phone she had invited a few friends to welcome Jack to the island, reeling off several names I was expected to recognise. I was tempted to ask if George was invited but assumed it a given. I was keen for Jack to get to know George.

I carried our plates of food out to the garden and Jack brought the bottle of wine, the one George had given to me. Jack cut the rim of the covering and then successfully removed the cork from its bottle. How do you know if a wine is top notch? I remembered a friend telling me that you are supposed to take a whiff of it first, so I placed the glass under the tip of my nose and breathed in the aroma.

'What are you doing?' Jack asked.

'Smelling the wine, isn't that what you're supposed to do?' Jack shrugged. I wasn't detecting a strong odour and I couldn't remember the next step.

I took my first sip and it tasted flavoursome, lingering on my palate. I was impressed having sampled a good selection in my time and suspected it wouldn't be cheap to buy. How would one go about buying a vineyard and how much do they cost to buy and perhaps George was well connected to people in this line of work. All of these questions filling my mind. Maybe that was the link to Stavros and they were business partners. Certainly an unusual occupation and I was keen to find out more.

Jack appeared preoccupied with his phone and I studied the landscape before me. There was a stillness to the night, not even a murmur from any insects.

An image of me and George on his moped came to mind as I hung on to his toned body, making our way back up the winding road. And remembering my surprise shock of finding out he owned a vineyard. A vineyard, I wasn't expecting to find that. Then jumping to his last comment that confirmed he wanted to go out with me again. Another date. Although Jack's arrival had put a spanner in the works, I still wanted to dedicate some serious time to research where I should go on my next adventure with George.

After our second glass of wine, Jack looked at me with one of his mischievous expressions and then asked, 'Do you think there will be anybody at Aella's gathering who is the same age as me?'

I suspected he was interested to know if Aella had invited any of her female friends. I wasn't sure she had that many as she didn't speak of them. I got the impression if she did, they were probably part of a couple and more likely acquaintances of Stavros.

'I really don't know, any reason why?'

Jack took a drink of his wine and then spoke. 'No reason, just hope they are not all older than me because I won't have anything in common with them.'

'Well since you are not staying too long, I'm sure you will survive one night being amongst us oldies,' I replied with a sarcastic tone. The cheek of him, I wasn't much older than him myself.

I finished my glass off, leaving Jack enough wine in the bottle for another glass for him. I made my excuses that I needed to get on with writing in the morning, especially as we were out to dinner the following night where more drink would be flowing.

Chapter 13

The following morning I made an early start and threw myself into achieving my quest before Jack made an appearance. I was pleased with the way my story was progressing and keen to keep my flow going. My main character the dashing archaeologist Thomas, had recently arrived in Marseilles shortly after the French Revolution in search of buried treasures. Thomas had a hidden past which I was slowly revealing to my readers. His character portrayed one thing, but the reality something very different.

    I am sure I wouldn't have had as much inclination to write if I'd stayed in England. Without doubt the weather here a great incentive, waking up to clear skies undeniably made me more motivated. I definitely didn't miss the unpredictability of the English climate. Snow, bitter wind and freezing rain hopefully in the distant past.

A couple of hours passed by and still no sign of Jack, so I left him sleeping. I seized my walk down to the water's edge, my little ritual, which I'd missed since Jack arrived. As the clear water cooled my feet George's image came to mind and I wondered if he would be at the dinner. Of course he would, he came across as a social animal. I thought about Nico and whether he was on his way to see me when Jack spotted him. Perhaps Nico didn't consider it appropriate to visit while Jack stayed with me or he could have been simply passing by.

I found Jack in the kitchen drinking coffee and nibbling on a bowl of fruit when I got back. By this time, it was getting close to midday and I told him that I was going to continue with my writing for another hour and then I would fix us both a light lunch. I didn't eat anything too heavy in the day.

'Don't worry about me, I think I might go into the town and take a look at where the bus routes might take me,' he stated.

'Okay, that sounds adventurous.'

Jack drank the last of his coffee. 'Don't want to get under your feet. Anyway, I feel like being adventurous today,' he said puffing out his chest.

'Make sure you put on plenty of sun cream, it is warm out there,' I told him, after all it was June. Unlike me Jack tanned easily, but even so you could never be too careful. People would probably find it hard to believe me and Jack were related as we didn't have any shared feature resemblances; his eyes brown, mine blue and grey, not to mention the obvious height difference.

'Yes dear sister, I will,' he said winking at me. That wink well perfected and had presumably made a number of women fall for his charm.

Jack left shortly after and I resumed my writing. I reasoned with Jack's arrival it may prevent me from achieving much, therefore his trip out gave me no excuse.

An hour after Jack departed I heard a buzzing noise. Five minutes later buzzing again. My curiosity got the better of me and I picked up the phone where it lay at the side of the fridge.

Then a ping and a message. "Are you ignoring me?" came the question from someone called Jess.

Ping again. "You are!"

Ping again. "Jack you better have a good excuse this time!!!"

'What have you been up to now?' I muttered and switched off his phone, I didn't need Jack's love life interrupting my flow.

Late afternoon and I was having a rest which I sometimes did, when I heard Jack's voice. I peeled myself off my bed and went down to join him.

Jack appeared in good spirit as he told me he managed to buy a local map and had gone on a bus journey to another town. There was a glow on his face that was for certain, although I wasn't convinced it was from the sun, more likely the beer I could smell on him.

From what I could gather he had hit a tourist spot and bumped into a couple of backpackers in a bar. The travellers were from Scotland somewhere near Edinburgh and of the female variety naturally. This their second stop apparently of island hopping around the Greek islands. I was relieved he hadn't invited them back and suggested they stay, although it wouldn't have surprised me. He did manage to get their phone numbers and proudly pointed to where they were written, although hardly readable, on the inside of his right arm. Never an opportunity lost with Jack.

'Your phone is by the fridge. I switched it off, it was distracting me.'

Jack's mouth opened wide and let out a huge yawn. 'I thought as much, good job I didn't get into any trouble, hey.'

Jack grabbed his phone and disappeared for a nap, while I delved into my sparse wardrobe once again, to see what I could conjure up for our upcoming dinner. It didn't occur to me before I came to live here I would be invited out to social gatherings. I'm not sure what I expected really, but I'd assumed because I was living in a small town and the fact I was English, I would be left to get on with my life and not much interaction with the locals. Not for a good while anyway. When I first arrived I knew I would stand out and anticipated stares, but surprisingly nobody appeared that interested even though I appeared to be the only English person living in the town. That was until I met George.

Most of the clothes and few pairs of shoes I brought with me were for casual wear (a lot of my formal clothes I had given to charity), but who would have presumed I would meet a socialite such as Aella.

I speculated what Aella would be wearing as I perched on the end of my bed, she always appeared to have a new item of clothing on whenever I met her. I was confident she didn't shop in the town because her clothes looked way more expensive. She had a fine selection of jewellery too, no doubt gifts from Stavros over the years. Whatever I wore would definitely be upstaged by her.

As I mentioned earlier, we first met at the market whilst both admiring the same vase one day. If I hadn't stopped to admire the vase I may never have met Aella and my life on the island could have started out differently I'm sure.

At one of our early coffee meets, which depending on how much Aella had to say could last some time, she informed me that her name meant storm wind; whirlwind. Apparently in Greek mythology this is the name for an Amazon warrior who was killed by Heracles. The Amazon warrior was known for wielding a double-axe. I wondered if Stavros was mindful of the meaning to her name.

'And what does your name mean?' she asked me.

'I have no idea,' I replied.

After Aella revealed the meaning of her name I became intrigued to find out if there was one behind mine, and as soon as I returned to my house I looked it up and it said "pure". I was disappointed to find this because clearly it wasn't as exciting as Aella's, but then again I guess it could have meant something a lot worse. I didn't tell Aella I looked it up, hoping she had forgotten the discussion.

And so I began to learn more about my new Greek friend. She told me that when she was first introduced to Stavros they happened to be at a family wedding. She already had a boyfriend at the time and a number of other admirers, yet this did not put Stavros off. The news he had competition did not deter Stavros and made him work harder to claim his prize. Aella knew as soon as she met Stavros he would be the man she would marry and enjoyed the extra effort he was putting in, wining and dining her and buying her gifts. When the inevitable happened and they did marry Aella never worked again, although I am not entirely convinced she ever did, the topic has never come up in conversation. Firstly, she didn't need to as Stavros was a wealthy man, so she had divulged to me. I deduced Aella would not have settled for a man who wasn't wealthy, she looked high maintenance. Secondly, he would not let her because he wanted her to be the mother of his children and that should be her primary focus. She accepted this condition certain she was not at all maternal. In fact she had no intention of becoming pregnant, consequently she secretly took contraceptive pills to ensure it didn't happen.

After two years of marriage, Stavros started to grow suspicious of why his wife was not carrying their child. Both their families too. Aella was running out of excuses as to what the problem could be, suggesting perhaps she was not able to have children and never putting the blame on her husband. And then following a stomach bug the unthinkable happened, Aella found herself pregnant. She told me how unhappy she had felt and did not tell Stavros at first. She considered having a termination and even went as far as booking the appointment but didn't have the courage to go through with it.

You see Aella had been pregnant before, she was only sixteen. Faidon was the father of the baby, her first true love and four years older than Aella. He was also the best friend of her brother. Aella's family never found out about her pregnancy because she had a termination. She confided in her aunt who sorted the arrangements, enabling Aella to keep her secret. Apparently Faidon was also popular amongst other girls in the town where Aella lived, she soon found out. It was the first and only time I saw a vulnerable side to Aella as she spoke, tears swelling in her eyes as she revealed to me her hidden secret.

A termination wasn't an option, it would have caused too much pain to both of their families if they found out, not to mention Stavros. Accordingly, she revealed to Stavros whom she loved very much he was to become a father and now they have a handsome boy called Stephon who is five years old. He is named after his grandfather (Stavros's late father) as is the Greek tradition. It was obvious they both doted on Stephon, I doubted Aella would have any more but you never knew with her.

Aella can wear anything and look gorgeous and I feel a bit inferior when I am in her presence. Not on an intellectual basis you understand, more in the beauty and sense of style department. She always appeared to get her outfit just right, never tarty and always classy. I often wondered how she kept her figure so trim too.

I let out a sigh as I sized up my pitiful collection. I left Jack peacefully sleeping and set off into town determined to find something to wear, coming back empty handed not an option, after all how hard could it be.

Chapter 14

I stopped by the church on my way into town delaying the task before me, hoping to see Nico, thinking I could squeeze in a quick hello.

Three young boys sat huddled under the large tree guarding the church. They looked my way, quietening their voices and continued with their mischief. Each had a stick in their hand and I couldn't see what poor creature they teased, a lizard perhaps.

The welcomed coolness hit my skin as I stepped through the wooden door. I found Nico inside. I sat on one of the benches at the rear of the church and lowered my head as if in prayer. I liked to think I looked convincing. I realised I'd never discussed my faith with Nico, he had never quizzed me about it, which was a good job as I wasn't sure I had one. Even though Jack and I were both christened as babies at the local church close to our family home. It seemed the fashionable thing to do in those days followed by a party. Obviously I can't remember it, being one at the time. It made me wonder who my god parents were, I can't remember ever being told or asking about them come to think of it. No point asking Jack, he would be clueless.

After a short time I became aware of somebody close to me. It was him, there was an aura about Nico I could sense. He had a pure smell about him too and I imagined he didn't lavish himself in fancy shower gel.

'Hello,' his voice just a whisper.

'Hi,' I whispered back.

I got up first and walked out of the church thinking it inappropriate to have a chat in a holy place. Nico followed me. I don't know why but my heart started racing, as if I were being chased by a tiger. Maybe a slight exaggeration.

We sat on a sun-parched bench against the side wall of the church, giving me time to take control of my breathing. I accepted I should start our conversation, after all I had come to search Nico out.

'Jack tells me he saw you pass my house yesterday,' I enquired.

'Yes,' he replied.

I crossed my arms. 'Why didn't you stop by and say hello?' I tried not to sound too disappointed.

'I visited a sick man who lives not far from where you live.'

'Oh,' I replied and there was me thinking he was on his way to visit me.

'He is unlikely to live much longer.'

I was about to ask what was wrong with the man and stopped myself.

'He is refusing to go to hospital and his family asked me to pray with them,' Nico added. Of course Nico would be doing that, and not on his way to visit an English woman who speculated he may like her as more than a friend. I uncrossed my arms.

'Nico, where do you live?'

'Live, why do you ask?'

'It's just whenever I see you, it is at the market, the church, or at my place drinking tea. I am curious.' I wish I hadn't been so direct.

'I live in the town of course.' How was I supposed to know that? He could have lived in another town for all I knew.

'I'm going into the town now to buy something, perhaps you could show me?'

'Okay,' he replied and didn't appear shocked by my directness, only a slight raise of his eyebrows.

Nico stood and started to walk in silence and I joined him. I was surprised he could abandon his work just like that.

As we approached the main square, it was quiet, as if sleeping whilst the market was not there. Nico halted and pointed to a side street. 'This way,' he said.

I became aware I had never ventured down this street before, the cobbled stones more uneven and darker in tone. Most of the houses were decorated with large hanging baskets, their contents spilling over with brightly coloured flowers for all to enjoy. No rubbish or debris could be seen as inhabitants took a sense of pride in their homes.

We soon arrived at a tall narrow house and a green door, sandwiched either side by houses of the same style but with different coloured doors. Each house with matching closed shutters, protecting their homes from the sun.

'Would you like to come in?' I was surprised Nico asked me such an obvious question.

'Yes, only if you have time.'

I couldn't quite believe he was actually asking me in, my heart started to race again and I hoped he couldn't see my chest rise and fall. I registered I shouldn't have been having these thoughts, as if a priest would be gaping at my chest. I glanced behind me to check nobody could see me entering his house before I followed him in.

Once inside, the house presented as it looked from the outside, quite narrow. On the left sat a small green sofa against a bare wall leading to a kitchen. Not much of social space and from there a spiral staircase led upwards. Nico climbed the stone stairs in silence and I followed.

The steps took us up to another level which led to a room on the right where a dark wooden door was closed. Then a few more steps to a further level to find another living space and a few items of furniture including a bookcase, desk and chair. I deduced the room below with the closed door was his bedroom.

'Please, come and sit out here.' Nico led me out onto a small shaded patio area which I presumed looked down onto the street from where we came from.

'Do you have time for tea?' he asked.

A quick glance at my watch, I certainly did. 'Yes that would be lovely.'

Nico returned back inside and down into his kitchen to make our tea (that must keep him fit I imagined), while I made myself comfortable on a cushioned bench and took in my surroundings. I breathed out a small sigh.

A long window box painted turquoise and

etched with Greek writing was secured to the white wall in front of me. Red and white flowers were in full bloom. I focussed in on the italic writing but had no idea what the words meant on the window box. Perhaps a religious quote? I'd been trying to learn some basic Greek words, keen to be accepted as a resident. In fact when Nico visited he would often test my conversation, just basic words to help me gain more confidence. I found it a challenging language to learn and didn't think about going to classes before I came to live here.

Although I found the outside area on the small side, Nico had made it welcoming. I wondered if he spent much time in this space, it was clearly tranquil. Luckily it wasn't overlooked by another property and only the faintest of sounds wafted up from the street below. Which was just as well, as I imagined he would need his privacy with being a priest and the things that priests do. His footsteps alerted me to his return.

'Here we are, I have no cake I was not expecting a visitor.' Nico's attempt at humour or maybe sarcasm. A vision of him in an apron and a mixing bowl came to mind.

Nico moved a chair closer to sit alongside me. I sipped on my hot tea, contemplating what to say, secretly wishing I was drinking a cold beer. At least that would have settled my nerves. Nico sensed my nerves, therefore he started the conversation.

'What do you think of my house?' he asked.

It appeared basic, but I chose to be diplomatic. 'It's very nice.'

'It is simple but it suits my needs, you are the first person to visit me.' Nico drank from his cup.

'Oh, I feel very honoured Nico.' I wondered if he had any friends on the island or perhaps I was his only one outside the church. I assumed Nico classed me as a friend.

After the initial embarrassment of my insistent request we chatted about Jack. Nico asking me a few questions but never prying. It was a skill of his I noticed and I did appreciate his generous listening.

'That's enough about Jack, I'm sure his ears are burning.'

'Ears are burning?' I found it hard to believe Nico hadn't heard this turn of phrase.

'It means someone is talking about you behind your back.'

'Behind your back?' I pondered whether Nico was teasing me at this point.

'Yes.' I nodded my head forward. 'Never mind it is an English saying.'

'I am learning some strange ways of the English.' Nico placed his hand to his chin and stared straight at me, daring me to continue.

I was quick to fire back. 'What about Greeks, they must have some strange sayings?'

'Let me think about that.' It didn't take him long. 'How about, the donkey called the rooster big headed.'

'And what does that mean?' I had to contain my laughter.

'Someone criticizes another person for a fault he has himself, of course.' Nico allowed himself a victorious smile. His eyebrows raised above the thick black lashes framing those dark brown eyes. Nico appeared to be in playful banter, so I took the opportunity to find out more about him.

'Why did you become a priest Nico?' My voice softer and more serious.

'Good question,' he replied and paused.

'Are you going to answer?'

'Yes.'

I was about to say 'I'm all ears' and corrected myself. 'I'm listening.' I waited eagerly for his tale.

'I dreamed of being a teacher as a boy. I worked hard at school, the smartest in my class.' Nico looked up to the clear blue sky as if searching for his next words.

'When I was fifteen years old, I became ill suddenly. My temperature very high and a rash covering my whole body. Eventually a doctor told my parents I had scarlet fever. I was very sick, my energy sucked out of me and it affected me so much I didn't return to my studies. It was an extremely dark time for me.' Nico's face stayed strangely emotionless even though this illness appeared to have had a profound effect.

'As I became stronger my uncle took me under his wing. He was a priest. He still is a priest. I spent many hours watching him at his work, during mass, visiting the sick, his selfless commitment to others, until it became a way of life for me too.'

I found myself hanging on his every word expecting him to continue and then he changed the subject.

'What were you coming to buy?'

'Sorry?'

'You were on your way into town.'

'Oh yes, I completely forgot.' I checked my watch and it was after 5pm, I'd run out of time to buy anything and I needed to get back to shower and ready myself for the dinner.

'Time to go?' he asked.

I sat forward on the seat, my body ready to make its move. 'Yes.'

I followed Nico back through the house and

down the stairs to his door. He was about to open the door when he took my hand in both of his. 'Thank you for visiting.'

Our bodies had never touched before, his hands pleasantly soft.

'I don't think you had much choice in the matter Nico.' And we both smiled together. Nico released my hand.

I opened the door and off I went with a spring in my step and a smirk on my face.

Chapter 15

I rooted around in my wardrobe. Right at the back I placed my hand on a dress I hadn't worn for some time. I definitely hadn't worn it since I'd lived here.

We were on our honeymoon in Antibes, and as we wandered around the trendy shops of the new town, Paul picked up a jade coloured dress hanging on a metal rail.

'Try this one on,' he said.

'It's too hot.'

'Go on.'

Reluctantly I stepped inside and disappeared behind the pink curtain of the small boutique shop. The material felt silky against my skin as I slipped the dress on. I looked into a floor standing mirror to find my shoulders exposed and a gently scooped neckline. The sides of the dress sat nicely on my hips and subtly kicked out to fall just below my knees.

'Come and show me,' Paul called out.

I pulled back the curtain and strutted out. I gave Paul a twirl and he nodded his head and gave me a thumbs up sign. I checked the price on the handwritten tag after I had taken it off.

'Far too pricey,' I told Paul, scrunching up my nose. It wasn't really, I didn't know when I would wear it.

'You're having it.' Paul took the dress from my hand and paid. I wore it that night on Paul's insistence.

The dress appeared to still fit, until I tried to pull the zip at the side and it was challenging. I had obviously put on a couple of pounds since I'd moved here, and I found this surprising, certain I'd been eating more healthily. It was feasible my increased alcohol consumption could be blamed or perhaps my metabolism was finally slowing down.

I huffed and puffed and realised I'd only gone and got the zip caught in the material. I had no way of getting the dress back off. Reluctantly I went downstairs.

'I'm stuck.'

'What do you mean?' Jack's eyebrows formed a frown.

'Here.' I turned sideways to reveal my exposed skin. Jack didn't say a word, he got up from the chair and quickly and proficiently sorted my problem.

'There, you scrub up alright sis.' I welcomed that as a compliment from Jack.

'Cheeky, you don't look too bad yourself,' I replied just as our ride arrived outside. It was definitely a perk being a friend of Stavros.

An older Greek couple happened to be the first people we talked to when we arrived. Jack was not being discreet, his eyeballs rolling from side to side. We attempted to make conversation with them, though their English extremely limited. Some others I recognised and registered they were Stavros's work colleagues along with their wives too. The men wore suits similar to Stavros, it appeared over the top, especially on a warm night such as this.

Aella made her entrance, floating into the room looking divine in one of her many captivating dresses, this one an olive green colour. I was thankful it wasn't the same colour green as mine, I knew I shouldn't compete with Aella.

Aella made a bee line for Jack straight away, sashaying across the room. She placed her hands on his shoulders, kissing him on both cheeks as if they were great friends. She turned to wink at me and mouthed, 'Nice dress.' And then took Jack's arm and whisked him off to introduce him to the other guests. I noticed Stavros observing the two of them from afar.

Left standing alone, I glanced around to see if George had arrived. I couldn't spot him, he was obviously running late after a busy day.

Stavros had made his way over to me. 'Looking for someone?'

'Stavros, where is George tonight?'

Sensing my expectation he replied, 'I'm sorry, he cannot be here tonight.'

'Oh, is he alright?' I was surprised to hear this from Stavros, I assumed George would be a regular fixture at their parties.

'Yes of course. A visitor has arrived at the airport.'

I thought back to when we arrived, expecting to be picked up by a lavish coach to transport us to our accommodation, only to find we had to get on a ferry to bring us to Kalymnos. Oh and not forgetting that bloody awful taxi ride. Thankfully the island had its own airport now.

'I didn't know he was expecting a visitor,' I replied.

'Neither did George. It is his daughter.' I felt the

weight of Stavros's arm around my shoulder and he gave me a gentle squeeze. 'Never mind you will have the pleasure of my company tonight.'

I looked up at Stavros's face. 'I am looking forward to it.'

We both chuckled. I did like Stavros, he showed kindness to me. I had a sense he was looking after me akin to an older brother. I guessed him to be older than Aella by about ten years.

I found parties with Stavros and Aella never too formal. Guests took their seats at a long wooden table inside the house, where upon a varied selection of Greek delights were displayed to tempt us. Wine was plentiful and I recognised the gold label on a couple of bottles from George's vineyard. I still found it astonishing he owned one.

I smiled and conversed but felt a bit flat. I hadn't known George very long, but I missed his presence, an energy he gave out effortlessly. Stavros sensed this, paying me extra attention while Aella had attached herself to Jack on the other side of the table. Oblivious to the other guests around them.

'Your brother is charming.' As he said this a frown appeared on Stavros's face.

'Yes too charming,' I replied and lifted the almost empty glass to my lips.

I sensed Stavros may have been somewhat jealous of the younger man chatting up his beautiful wife. Probably wasn't the first time he had observed another man be enchanted by Aella. Luckily for Stavros, Aella was very loyal and enjoyed the game of flirting. She appreciated she would not find a finer man than in Stavros. I assumed Stavros knew that.

I said I first met Aella at the market, my introduction to Stavros came a month later. I got the impression he was always kept busy by his work. One day I had the honour of meeting him because he ventured into the town with Aella. This was apparently unlike him. Aella had made it known to her husband she had a met a new friend who was a writer and he must come and meet her. That friend was me of course.

When we met, Stavros was just as I imagined him from Aella's description: tall, dark and handsome as the cliché goes and carrying a bit of extra weight around his middle. He presented himself as confident and charismatic. Stavros appeared interested to hear about my life before living on the island, his questions probed though didn't feel intrusive. He didn't appear to be in a rush to leave my company and it became evident he was suitably read up on English history, with a specific interest in Tudor times and Henry the VIII. Aella sat quietly, possibly bored, unable to contribute while her husband held court with his new acquaintance.

As we sat and drank our coffee, it became apparent Stavros was familiar to a number of people, young and old who stopped to greet him as they passed by. Strange thoughts came to mind. I contemplated if he could be the head of a Greek mafia or perhaps a shipping magnate, Aella had never divulged what he did for a living, just that he was a businessman. I endeavoured on a couple of occasions to ask Aella about Stavros's work but she always steered me off the subject, which intrigued me more. Perhaps he had a number of business ventures some of which Aella may not have known of. She never complained about him being busy, it was obvious he provided well for his family.

I took to Stavros straight away and him to me. Aella used to tease me that Stavros had a soft spot for me, my observation was he appeared like this with everyone. However, I am not denying I wasn't flattered Aella had paid me this compliment. If ever I befell trouble, the romantic in me imagined I could count on Stavros to be my knight.

The sound of music filled the room, the volume gradually getting louder. Stavros needed no encouragement and pulled me to my feet, his love for dancing shown on his smiling face as he moved his body to the rhythm. Others joined us including Aella and Jack. A large circle formed and the loud noise of clapping hands rang out.

Stavros pulled Aella into the centre, his hands clasping hers twirling her elegant figure around. We were next, Jack spinning me excitedly around as if we were two kids on a fairground ride. It was good fun and I forgot all about George and my visit to Nico's earlier.

Guests started to depart as the evening came to a close. Some needing more help than others to leave. I had drank my fair share of wine and Jack looked worse for wear, his body gently swaying. Time to call it a night and Stavros arranged for the same driver to take us home.

Chapter 16

My morning writing went out of the window. I didn't wake until 10am, most unlike me and I put it down to the amount of wine I consumed the night before. Since Jack arrived, I'd been drinking a lot more alcohol than I was used to in recent times.

I made my way down to the kitchen and made a pot of coffee, assuming Jack would surely be in need, recalling a thudding sound as he stumbled up the stairs. I decided I would take the day off and spend it with my brother should he choose to wake at a reasonable hour.

I stepped out into the garden, coffee in hand and tuned in to a hissing noise and had no idea what insect was communicating, not the familiar sound of cicadas. George's face appeared as I gave up trying to locate the hidden insect. So, Millie had arrived. I guessed George must have been extremely pleased to see her, even if he wasn't expecting her. I remembered him telling me she would be visiting at some point. George's situation not too different to my own occurring in my mind. I wondered how long she would be visiting for and if we might get to meet her as I returned back indoors.

Jack eventually stirred around eleven, as I was thinking of cooling my feet in the sea. His hair sticking up and out in all directions but still looking handsome.

'Coffee?'

'Water first.' He stuck out his tongue like a panting dog, forcing me to smile, and then rested his head on his folded arms.

I poured water into a glass and placed a packet of paracetamol next to it. Jack looked as though he might need them.

'Did you enjoy the party?' I asked him.

'It was surprisingly good, especially the wine,' he said, lifting his head and massaging his head.

'Yes, you certainly put plenty of that away.' No shock to me he was hung over and I wasn't feeling too sharp myself.

'I did spot it was the same one we had the other night.'

'Yes, from George's vineyard,' I told him.

Jack took a moment to register what I'd said, a puzzled look forming.

'He has his own vineyard?'

'Yes, I thought I'd told you.' It wasn't something I had purposefully kept from him.

'You absolutely did not, well isn't he just the catch.'

'Jack, we are just friends.' My voice louder than normal emphasising my point.

'So you say.' Jack reverted back to massaging his head.

'Anyway, let's get you some breakfast, although it's nearly lunchtime.'

That day we succumbed to a leisurely pace. Jack appeared quite happy to hang around and see off his hangover. Later in the afternoon we ambled along the sea front barefoot, playfully flicking water at each other. Reminding me again of our summer holidays in Cornwall when we were younger. Of course back then I was not only the oldest but also taller than Jack. I was very much in charge bossing him around and making him do what I wanted to do. A memory popped up of him pulling me around in our dingy while I lay back enjoying the ride. I hoped he didn't recall how mean I was to him.

We sat on the coarse sand.

Stretching my legs out, I turned to my brother. 'Jack, can you believe you have been here almost a week.'

Jack sat forward his arms resting on his knees as he looked out across the sea. 'I know, I'm surprised to say I'm quite enjoying myself.'

'That's good to hear.'

Jack picked up a handful of sand and watched the grains fall through his fingers. 'It beats the fast pace of life in London. I can see why you like it here.'

'What do you think you will do when you get back home?'

He looked up to meet my eyes. 'Not sure. Probably sounds silly but I did envy those backpackers I met the other day. Wish I was brave enough to do something as adventurous as that.'

'Why not, you have the money to do it.' He hadn't told me what his financial situation was but I assumed he received a decent payout when he left his job.

'Maybe I'm too old now.' He sounded quite serious and not the playful Jack I knew.

Jack turned his face away from me, I couldn't read the emotion on his face. I felt sorry for him, perhaps he found himself at a crossroads in his life and I hadn't picked up on the signs.

I tried to lighten the atmosphere. 'Since when is there an age limit?'

'Hmm.' Jack raised his eyebrows as he looked my way. 'Trying to get rid of me are you?'

'No, of course not.'

'Good. Anyhow, I don't want to make any rash decisions,' he replied. He had a point he was on holiday after all and didn't appear to have any ties back home; on the work front.

Jack changed the subject. 'Shall I bury you in the sand?' He was referring to the photo I had left for him.

'Perhaps another day,' I replied with a smile.

Not long after we returned to the house I popped outside to water my plants, the flowers still flourishing. When I stepped back inside Jack was rummaging around in the kitchen cupboards, opening and closing doors and I suspected he was searching for beer, the fridge now empty. He soon departed to the town to stock up.

When he arrived back he was armed with two bags, one containing beer and out of the other one he took two pieces of fish and placed them on the worktop. He didn't offer to cook and instead stood watching me season them as he opened a bottle of beer. His hangover long gone it would appear.

That night after dinner in the garden, Jack suggested we play cards. I was surprised he had brought some with him. I was rubbish at cards as I recalled playing with Paul and would often get in a huff when he won every game hands down. It became a standing joke between us. I was hoping Jack wasn't a card shark and I might win a game or two.

'I thought George would have been at the party last night,' Jack said, placing the queen of diamonds on the table. Somehow I had forgotten to tell my brother the news.

'I forgot to tell you, Stavros told me George called him before the party. George's daughter has arrived and he went to pick her up.'

'What? Out of the blue.' The irony of Jack.

'Seems that way.' I picked up the queen of diamonds and placed down the five of spades.

'How old is his daughter?'

I didn't look up at Jack's face, my eyes fixed on my hand of cards.

'I don't know how old she is, but she has been to university recently. Rummy.' I placed my cards down and grinned at my brother.

Jack's eyebrows raised astonished I won so quickly.

'Beginners luck,' he said. He scooped up the cards, gave them a quick shuffle and placed them between us. My deal.

I won the next two games before he managed to beat me.

Chapter 17

The early morning sun brought my bedroom to life. I lay in my bed thinking of George. What a surprise he'd had. Selfishly I considered whether we would get to go on another outing together now that he had his visitor. Be patient Kate, I told myself, confident George was a man of his word, no evidence to suggest otherwise. And perhaps when I saw him next he would fill me in, convinced our paths would cross soon. In the meantime I had my own visitor to keep me occupied.

To my amazement Jack was already up, showered and dressed sitting at the kitchen table. Unaware of my arrival, he carried on singing along to the tune playing in his ears. I have to say his voice sounded pretty good, another one of his attributes to sell to the ladies.

Day six for Jack and I couldn't believe he'd been here almost a week. I was getting use to my new lodger especially as he wasn't under my feet all day. I made my presence known and Jack removed the white ear phones.

'Reckon I might go on another adventure today, fancy coming with me?'

'I would love to dear brother, but I must crack on if I am to meet my deadline.'

'Your loss,' Jack stated.

'Perhaps another day.'

I was expecting a call from Janet to check how I was progressing. She didn't appear to be an organised person and as a result of this a specific date had not been agreed. 'I'll contact you at the end of June,' she'd said.

I wanted to give her good news when she did make contact, after all she had taken a chance on me. And, after she got over the initial shock about me leaving the country, she appeared intrigued and full of admiration I had taken such a bold step. She made me promise to send her some snaps so she could visualize me in my new setting. I did just that along with the chapter I'd been working on. 'Very tranquil' she wrote back, I assumed she referred to Kalymnos and not my writing because that was not the genre of my book.

Deciding I must make the most of the time I had

alone to write, assuming Jack would be back by late afternoon, I was hit with writer's block. I typed writer's block into the search engine and the first suggestion: "Go for a Walk". I'm surprised I didn't come up with that myself.

I grabbed my hat and stepped out. Instead of heading off to my usual spot or going left into town I ventured right, a fairly barren route if honest and the radiant heat was making itself known. Stupidly I hadn't brought anything to drink and my throat was in need of lubrication, a juicy ice lolly would have done the trick. Ordinarily, I was surprised how easily I had adapted to a warm climate (I suspect my doubters didn't think I would last long), but when you live in such a place you don't tend to sunbathe!

Drawn back to the sight of the glistening sea, I spotted a white shape and could just make out the outline of a boat in the distant water. I perched on a large rock.

Who was on board? Perhaps someone rich and famous. Where was it bound as it sat motionless in the deepness of the sea? I was wishing I owned binoculars to get a closer look, another purchase I should look into. Nevertheless the sight of the boat gave me an idea for a new angle and I registered the thought and made my way back, ready to start work again.

Jack eventually rolled in at seven accompanied by the trudging sound of his feet on the tiled floor.

'Good day?' I asked.

'Yes, but I'm exhausted the heat got to me today.' He flopped down and kicked his huge trainers off.

'You get used to it,' I replied.

'Really?' Jack didn't sound convinced. 'I think I need to invest in a hat.'

'Good idea, doubt mine will suit you.' Jack didn't respond. 'Why don't you take a shower it might revive you, after you can tell me all about your travels.'

'Think I will.' Jack managed to haul himself up.

Jack didn't resurface again, I'd popped upstairs to find his door closed and gently opened it. I found him fast asleep, his breathing loud, clearly done in by the day's events. Jack didn't have a care in the world and what a great situation to be in. I returned downstairs and poured a generous glass of red wine.

I picked up a book from the limited selection I owned, bought not long after I came here and headed out into the garden. I was fortunate enough to come across a small book shop in the town quite early on. The lady owner resembled a pantomime dame, she had died auburn hair piled on top of her head and large hazel eyes sat beneath drawn on eyebrows arching high and wide. Several gold chains decorated her neckline and rings on every finger as she stood at the entrance to her doorway. She said something in Greek and then French, recognising I was European though not immediately English until I corrected her. She had a kind plump face and a gentle smile. I followed her inside, intrigued to see what I might find.

She returned to her chair and let me peruse the different sized books, some piled in a disorderly fashion on tables and others on dusty shelves. I noted she sold both new and used books and then a glossy front cover caught my eye; a picture of a rugged coast line and deserted beach, surrounded by the sea. 'Welcome to the island of Kalymnos' it stated. Luckily for me it was written in English. I picked it up and scanned the contents page to find it included places to visit, the island's history, culture and that sort of thing. I stepped out of the shop with my new purchase.

There was no reason I could think of why I couldn't make a start on planning my outing with George, (or as he put it, our next adventure) even if it didn't happen immediately. I flicked through the pages, hoping something might leap off a page to inspire my choice as I finished off the last of my wine. There appeared plenty of places of interest I had yet to see and I had a hunch George hadn't either. Rubbing my eyes, I let out a loud yawn and without any decision made I placed the book down and retired to my bed.

Chapter 18

I decided to treat Jack to an old favourite for breakfast, a boiled egg with soldiers. Recalling how Jack would always take the top of his egg off with great accuracy, and after eating the contents of the egg place its shell upside down as if it hadn't been touched.

Jack wasn't in his room when I looked in, therefore I assumed I would find him in the kitchen. No sign of him there either. He couldn't have gone far, he would have left me a note if he'd ventured further. Sure enough he waltzed in five minutes later.

'Where have you been?' I asked suspiciously.

Sweeping his locks back casually from his face. 'I've been for a swim.'

'Really?' I questioned his reply. His hair didn't look wet. Perhaps he had snuck off to meet the striking young waitress from the taverna. He had ample opportunity to organise a rendezvous while I chatted to the owner and settled our bill. Or maybe he was replying to the text messages he'd received, I suspected there were more.

'Yes really, I left my towel outside to dry,' he said plonking down at the table. Jack in his favoured seat and me in mine, we had assumed our places since his arrival like a married couple.

'I'm going to make your favourite breakfast,' I announced changing the subject.

'Oh yes what's that?'

'Boiled egg with soldiers.'

'Ha, I haven't had that since I was a child. Sounds good.'

'Thought it might bring back fond memories.'

'If you say so,' he said.

As the bubbles formed I placed the eggs in the saucepan and flipped the small glass timer over. Jack helped too by getting out the plates and egg cups. I switched on the radio and we sat to eat our eggs and soldiers, which I had neatly presented just like mum used to do. She wasn't the best of cooks but somehow managed to get this particular task exactly right, aided by her trusted timer. Mine never let me down, such a brilliant invention. I didn't own up to Jack I was quite partial to a boiled egg on a regular basis. In one of my reflective moments I contemplated acquiring a few chickens as I liked the idea of having fresh eggs on tap. Of course it was just a thought and I didn't get any further than that.

'So, what did you get up to yesterday that tired you out?'

Jack took off the top of his egg with purpose. 'This and that.'

'Really and it took all day did it?'

Jack's eyes remained on his egg. 'Just another bus journey to another place on the island.'

'What was it called this place?' Determined to find out where he had been.

Jack didn't respond and placed his crust on the pile with the others. It appeared quite odd that a man of his age would do such a thing. Perhaps he'd done this as a child and I had forgotten. I always ate my crusts and believed what my dad told me. 'Eat them all up Kate and you will grow curly hair, just like your mum.' And I did.

'Something beginning with a P,' he replied, his eyes still focused on his plate.

'Pothia, the capital?'

'Sounds about right,' he replied as if he couldn't be bothered to chat, placing the empty egg shell upside down in its cup. How could you not remember where you had been. And the capital of the island too.

It was obvious Jack didn't want to talk about his day out. This the moodier side to Jack showing through, I sensed he may be hiding something from me. I wouldn't have been surprised to find out he had settled in a bar for most of the day.

After breakfast we headed into town as I'd been summoned to meet Aella for coffee. Jack wasn't talkative, preoccupied with something while we walked. I left him to his thoughts.

We found Aella already waiting for us at her usual table. I doubted anybody else would have dared sit there, especially if they knew the true meaning of her name. She waved as we approached.

'You are looking much tanned Jack, it suits you,' Aella said fluttering her long eyelashes and patting the chair beside her, placing herself between us two.

'Thank you Aella,' he replied coyly, seating himself next to Aella. Jack's mood changed in an instance.

I had barely taken my seat when she fired straight at me. 'Kate, it is a shame George couldn't make it the other night.' Her hand resting on her chin, her eyebrows raised. Was Aella asking me my thoughts or making an obvious statement.

I picked up a menu with no intention of ordering food. I didn't reply straight away on purpose knowing the suspense would be agonising for Aella. Then I looked at her. 'Yes it was.'

Aella exhaled sharply. 'Perhaps we will meet his daughter soon. I wonder if she looks like George.'

'Perhaps,' I replied calmly.

'I'm looking forward to meeting her,' Jack piped up. Just as the words came out of Jack's mouth, Aella flashed me a quick look, her eyes widened in surprise.

Aella stood and waved. I turned my head as George approached through the stone archway. He was flanked either side by not one visitor but two.

'Good morning,' George said, his voice flatter than usual. We three remained silent.

George cleared his throat. 'This is my daughter Millie and my,' George hesitated '…wife Sarah.' George made no attempt to make eye contact with me as he directed his speech at Aella. Just as well, my eyebrows felt they had shot up two inches in surprise.

Aella never one to hold back, introduced herself first and then us. We were both lost for words allowing Aella to be our spokesperson.

'Would you care to join us?' Aella graciously

said. What was she thinking?

'Yes that would be lovely,' Sarah replied.

A game of musical chairs proceeded. Jack leapt up from his seat and gave up his chair for Sarah so that she was now sitting next to Aella, and directly opposite me. Millie stayed standing playing with a strand of her hair, while Jack grabbed a chair from the next table so she could sit alongside her mother. Jack grabbed two more chairs from another table, squeezing them in. George stood still while my brother carried out his self-assigned duty. Jack sat in the chair next to Millie leaving only one seat left, next to me. George last to sit down. I didn't glance his way, my glare focussing on my brother but he wasn't looking my way.

Aella called the waiter over who was loitering with intent. His hair greased back, giving his face a somewhat older look to his young years. More coffee was ordered as it appeared we were supposed to settle in with our new guests. At this point I felt like I was having an out of body experience, or perhaps a knockout blow more realistic. I sat motionless. George was married!

My eyes were drawn towards Millie, petite, cute, and fair-haired like George. Then reluctantly across to Sarah, a slightly bigger version of her daughter and brunette with a sharp cut shiny bob. I noticed Sarah's perfectly shaped finger nails painted in a bright red varnish as she placed her designer sunglasses into an expensive looking handbag. A square silver label shone in a prominent position displaying the designer's logo. Sarah was attractive and well-groomed unlike yours truly. Maybe that was what George liked about me, a more casual approach? Or maybe not, had I read the signs of attraction so very wrong. I glanced down at my shapeless bare nails.

'So, how long are you both staying for on our delightful island?' Aella asked of Sarah. My eyes drawn back towards my friend.

'We haven't decided. Millie has been taking some time out since graduating.' Sarah turned her head towards her husband. 'We are exceedingly proud of her, aren't we George.' I didn't glance at George to see his response but I assumed he nodded in agreement. 'She has a couple of job offers,' Sarah continued, 'and wanted to take a short break to consider her options. Isn't that right Millie?'

Millie and Jack were staring at each other intently. It was embarrassing.

'Millie.' Sarah repeated her daughter's name.

'Yes.' I don't think she heard what her mother said.

The coffees arrived and were placed on the table by the young waiter, his eyes widening when he saw Millie. Who could blame him as he took in the view of the pretty fair young women displayed before him. A rare sight in these parts. I glanced across at Jack's face and he looked displeased that someone dared to gaze at Millie whilst in his company, quite ridiculous they had only just met.

George was quiet and seemingly satisfied for Sarah to be their group's new spokesperson. If he had dared glance my way, my body language clear as I sat resembling a statue made of stone.

Finally George spoke his tone flat. 'Yes lots to discuss in the next couple of days.'

Nobody responded straight away. I found I had nothing to contribute to the conversation, taking prolonged sips from my coffee cup. I didn't even want another one and this one tasted too bitter.

I glanced Aella's way and she widened her eyes as if to prompt me to say something. I wasn't intentionally being silent, I couldn't think of anything appropriate to say. 'Sarah did you know your husband has been taking out another woman' in the forefront of my mind.

We could nevertheless, always count on Aella. 'I hope you are still coming to celebrate tomorrow George?'

'Celebrate?' George replied.

Aella raised her brows. 'You haven't forgot it is Stavros's birthday? In fact you and your guests are most welcome.' Aella threw her arms out wide to emphasise the point.

I had forgotten about the party myself with Jack arriving. I looked at my brother and he had a smug smile on his face after Aella's announcement. I wonder why?

'Thank you Aella.' Sarah turned her head towards her daughter. 'We would love to come.' And then added, 'If that's okay with you George?' Now looking at her husband through doe-eyes.

'I guess so,' George replied.

Sarah picked up her coffee cup using her left hand. How I could have missed them before is astounding. On Sarah's wedding finger she wore a white gold band, sitting above it a diamond solitaire engagement ring, the stone the size of a five pence piece and a sparkle I hadn't seen the like before. She looked my way and smiled and I smiled back, embarrassed she had caught me staring.

Sarah opened her mouth to say something just as Aella's driver arrived at the table to collect her. By far the quickest coffee date I had ever encountered with Aella and surprised she wasn't tempted to stay and interrogate Sarah further.

'I will have to leave you lovely people now,' Aella said.

'Already?' Sarah asked.

Aella lifted her hair expertly and shook the strands out to settle on her shoulders. 'I have a party to organise and there is still much to do.' Aella departed.

Still feeling perturbed by the scenario, I looked towards Jack and managed to catch his eyes. I tilted my head a fraction to the left, hoping he would gather my drift.

'We will need to make a move too,' I announced as I stood.

'Oh,' Sarah replied, her lips formed into a pout.

'I have some writing to do.'

'Yes. Kate is writing a book,' George added. Why he felt he needed to impart this information on my behalf I had no idea.

'How fascinating, I've never met an author before.' Sarah fixed her eyes on her daughter. 'How about that Millie?' Millie nodded and Jack reluctantly got up from his seat.

'Good to meet you both.' All I could muster and I couldn't look at George, even though I sensed he was looking at me.

'See you at the party Millie,' Jack said overly keen. He had turned into a love struck teenager in my opinion.

We walked away, my teeth clenched and I expected Jack to make a sarcastic comment. However, I think he was taken aback as much as me, were my initial thoughts.

'Think I will buy a new shirt for the party,' he eventually said.

'Good luck with that, probably won't find anything up to your usual standards here,' I remarked flippantly.

'I'll be the judge of that. I'm finding this place surprises me more and more each day I'm here,' he announced. Ditto I thought, my initial shock from Sarah's arrival had now turned into anger but I kept it in check with some restraint.

Chapter 19

As Jack left me, I had a sudden urge to knock on Nico's door now that I knew where he lived. I needed a friendly face to calm my inflamed mood. I glanced at my watch and suspected there was a strong chance he wouldn't be there, seeing that it was now late morning. Most likely he would be at the church or visiting sick people. I knocked anyway.

The door opened more swiftly than I expected. 'Hello, what a nice surprise.'

'I was just having coffee with friends and thought I'd say Hi.'

I found myself rooted to the spot not knowing if he were going to ask me in and then he replied, 'I saw you, I passed by a few moments ago.'

'Oh, you should have come over and said hello,' I quickly added.

Nico's face showed no emotion. I wasn't even aware if he drank coffee, I had only ever seen him drink tea.

'Where are my manners, please come in,' he said.

Glad to be invited in after a quick glance to the left and right, I couldn't get the bizarre experience over coffee out of my head. I told Nico who the people were but not too much detail, I didn't want him to think me a gossip. I couldn't remember if I had made Nico aware of my friendship with George, it had never come up in conversation. I certainly hadn't informed George about Nico. Well there wasn't anything to tell either of them, they were just my friends. Although, rightly or wrongly the idea that one could have been more before George's unexpected arrival, the other totally out of my reach.

'Would you like a cool drink?' he asked.

'Yes,' I replied nodding.

I followed him into his compact kitchen. No hint of a detectable odour and spotless, unlike mine, and I wondered if he did his own cleaning or if he had help. I waited while Nico poured juice from a carton into two tall glasses and then he led the way up the spiral staircase.

Before we stepped outside onto the patio area, I noticed two silver framed photographs on the bookcase I hadn't spotted during my previous visit. I deduced the people in one picture were of his parents. The other a female on her own.

Nico sat on the cushioned bench.

'Please sit with me,' he said, patting the space beside him.

I glanced at the chair he sat on the last time I visited, still positioned in the same spot. I viewed this as progress, that he seemed more at ease with my visit on this occasion.

Nico put the glass to his lips and drank slowly and I sat beside him.

'Nico, do you miss not being married?' Where did that come from, conscious mind not in control.

Nico was strangely calm when he replied, as if it were an everyday question. 'No, I do not Kate.'

I could have stopped there but I didn't. 'Have you ever had a relationship with a woman?'

'Lots of personal questions today.'

'Just curious.' Had I gone too far? I looked away wanting the ground to swallow me up.

'When I lived in Athens I did have a girlfriend. She wanted to get married and start a family and I was not ready for that important commitment.' He didn't look at me as he spoke, and stayed focussed on the window box in front of us. 'I used to meet with her in secret in the local park. I had to, my family wanted me to become a priest and I had already started on my journey to becoming one.' He took another drink. 'I struggled with the decision to choose the church over her for quite some time.' Nico paused and looked at me. 'Eventually I came to realise I had made the right decision. She met someone else and they married so my brother told me. They have a grown up daughter too.' Nico forced a smile.

I nodded in recognition.

He turned his gaze back to the window box. 'I asked to come and work here, to ensure no further distractions.'

I should have left it at that, satisfied he had shared more of his previous life with me.

'And do you find that you don't have any distractions here?' Not certain where I was going with this but keen to find out his answer, I waited for his reply.

Nico turned to me and I encountered the intensity of his dark brown eyes, our bodies motionless as if trapped in a moment of time. He looked away as if ashamed. I couldn't move, the tension between us unexpected and then he turned his face back to me. He leaned forward slightly and I felt his gentle touch as he cupped my chin in his hand.

I closed my eyes and the fullness of his lips were placed on mine.

'Does that answer your question?' His breath warm on my face, only inches separating us.

I felt a familiar sensation as my face started to flush and quickly averted my gaze to the ground. A need to steady my breathing, a chance to calm my racing pulse. At the same time wanting him to kiss me again. Nico removed his hand sensing my confused state.

'Right, better be on my way then, Jack will wonder where I have got to.' Lacking the courage to find out what would have happened next. 'Thanks for the drink.'

I couldn't get out of there fast enough, my emotions conflicting. Embarrassed I had let Nico kiss me, yet secretly wanting more. I flew down the stairs and didn't look back as I left his house, hastily turning the corner into one of the main streets.

'Hey, where's the fire?'

'Hi Jack, still shopping?'

'I reckoned you had gone back to the house.'

I had to think of a quick reply. 'I bumped into one of Aella's friends.' Sounded plausible. I looked down at the bag in his hand. 'What have you bought?'

'I have purchased a shirt as it happens, rather brighter than I would normally wear.' Jack pulled out a lilac coloured shirt from the bag and held it against his torso. 'What do you think?'

'It will suit you Jack.' I was never a fan of lilac, after being made to wear it as a bridesmaid, but sure Jack could carry the colour off.

'Do you mean that or are you still in shock from the fire?'

'Stop teasing Jack. Anyway I need a new dress too, fancy choosing something for me?' I was confident Aella would be wearing an attractive number and come to think of it Sarah too. Reluctantly deciding I should make the effort but if brutally honest I was thinking of faking an illness, a stomach bug sounded genuine enough. I didn't want to go to the party and act as if I were jubilant with Sarah's arrival and George's lack of integrity. The thought of seeing them together stirring up unwanted emotion within me, I had started to grow feelings for George.

Luckily there weren't many clothes shops to choose from, just as well as I wasn't one for browsing and trying extremely hard not to think about my kiss from Nico. It felt like my second out of body experience in just one day! Hence, nothing caught my eye until I decided on a navy halter neck dress with small polka dots, more adventurous than my usual choices. I took a gamble on it fitting, I couldn't be bothered to try it on. I had a pair of tan coloured sandals that pretty much went with anything, my outfit sorted.

Jack chose a cerise number from the selection and had a go trying to convince me it would suit me, but as I stood in front of the mirror and held the dress against me I wasn't convinced. I stuck with my original choice. Unlike Jack I did not want to make a statement that said 'check me out'. I doubted anyone would notice what I was wearing anyway, especially George. What a mess.

Jack appeared in a chirpy mood on our way back to the house.

'I'm starving, aren't you?' he asked.

I should have been, I hadn't eaten since breakfast. I wasn't sure I could stomach much food.

'I guess I could eat something,' I managed to reply.

Back at the house I rustled up some pasta and salad. Jack grabbed two beers from the fridge and headed out to the garden suggesting we play cards again.

'Are you going to finish that?' Jack asked. I had managed a few mouthfuls and hardly touched the salad. Jack didn't pick up on my change of mood.

'You have it, I'm watching my weight.' I patted

my stomach. Jack grabbed my plate and didn't respond.

I put on a convincing show I was concentrating on my cards as he won every game. Even his smug grin didn't get me riled.

Chapter 20

The evening of Stavros's party was upon us and my anxiety about seeing Sarah and George together was ramping up. During the day I was determined to finish a crucial chapter but was having flashbacks to my encounter with Nico. I eventually convinced myself that I was reading too much into the scene that played out at his house and he had got a bit carried away with the moment. On reflection, I certainly got carried away with my line of questioning.

We sat at my kitchen table enjoying a pre party drink.

'What's up with you, a bit quiet aren't we?' says Jack.

I glanced down at my wedding ring. 'Am I?'

'Upset George's wife has arrived?' I hadn't actually told Jack that I liked George but perhaps I implied something in the way I spoke of him.

My eyes fixed back on my brother. 'Ha ha Jack, he should be so lucky to have two women fighting over him.' I wasn't convinced I was ever a contender. It didn't help that Sarah was so damned attractive. That they were such a damned attractive couple. My emotions awakened again, still confused and angered why George hadn't mentioned his wife before. I didn't want to know, yet also wanting to know what story transpired there.

Our conversation cut short by the sound of a car engine outside, Stavros had sent a driver to pick us up for the party. Jack knocked back the rest of his drink, I didn't finish mine.

We climbed in the car.

'I wonder if Millie is already there.' Jack sounded keen.

'She is pretty, I suspect she may be popular.' I couldn't resist a little tease. Jack gave me a disapproving stare as if to say you should know better. 'I hope she appreciates your new shirt.'

Jack tugged at the collar of his lilac shirt. 'Who could resist me in this?' Or the strong scent of aftershave I noted. I didn't respond but managed a smile for my overly confident brother.

When we arrived, we made our way through the house and outside as we were to celebrate in the garden on this occasion. The theatre had been set and looked enchanting. White table cloths covered tables and a kaleidoscope of flowers took centre stage on each. Candles lit up glass lanterns hanging from branches of the large trees, casting shadows on the ground beneath. And caterers had been hired in for the big occasion too, with waiting staff balancing silver trays as they mingled with appetizers to tempt guests. It certainly was an impressive sight and I was amazed Aella hadn't spoken of what she had been up to.

'Wow,' Jack exclaimed. The last time we visited the house Jack didn't get chance to view the garden area.

I gave him a moment until speaking. 'Shall we.'

Jack linked his arm in mine as I led the way to the steps and then down a central path towards an impressive stone goddess. The elegant figurine stood in prime position, elevated on a raised patio area. The volume of voices increased as we approached the chatting guests, a few people glanced our way.

I spotted Stephon first, looking handsome in his suit matching his father's. Stephon jumped up and down a bundle of energy vying for Stavros's attention. Aella stood next to her husband wearing a cream lace dress, her hair neatly pinned up displaying an elegant neck and pearl drop earrings. Anyone could have easily mistaken the party for a wedding celebration.

Looking around the gathering it appeared the usual suspects had been invited and also family members. Aella had told me that their families met on many an occasion and there was rarely a crossed word. I didn't think to ask Aella how old Stavros was going to be. I assumed it a special birthday, because of all the trouble they had gone to, although he didn't look fifty. I regretted not buying a present when I spotted a table piled high with gifts. When I asked Aella later she replied, 'Not special, we do this for every birthday in our family.'

George arrived half an hour later along with his entourage. Talk about making an entrance, he looked exceptionally handsome in his light grey suit and then my eyes landed on Sarah. As I predicted she did not disappoint, striking, dressed in a jumpsuit which appeared navy too! Now wishing I'd chosen a different colour, not wanting to be in a fashion competition. It didn't help that Sarah had the shiniest hair I have ever seen and not a hair out of place, how did she manage that in this heat? I was slightly jealous of her glossy neat bob. Actually not slightly, extremely jealous. I had left my hair down and regretted it, the back of my neck clammy. Sarah didn't have that problem, her hair in a different league to mine.

My eyes moved to Millie. She carried off a figure hugging pink dress cut just above the knee. It suited her. I was thankful I hadn't been persuaded by Jack to buy the cerise number. I turned to speak to Jack, he'd disappeared and within a flash he appeared by Millie's side. Yes that name suited him Flash Jack, in his newly acquired lilac shirt.

I felt a slight touch on my shoulder. 'Don't you think it is strange George hasn't mentioned her before?' Aella said.

I let out the air from my lungs. 'That is an understatement Aella.' The mystery continued if indeed there was one.

Sarah was pointing in our direction and then they walked our way. They looked a striking couple together, their strides synchronized, a sign that they were unified. Sarah looked up at George with adoring affection and said something but he didn't turn his face to hers or reply.

As they got closer my brain told me to move but my feet were set in concrete.

'Aella, thank you for inviting us,' Sarah said as she approached. So, they were an 'us'. George lent forward to kiss Aella on both cheeks and completely ignored me.

As if Aella could sense my discomfort she spoke first, 'George thank you for coming, you must introduce Sarah to Stavros he is over by the statue.' Aella pointed to where Stavros was surrounded by some of his guests, keen to move them away, not allowing Sarah to start up a conversation.

As they turned and walked away George looked over his shoulder and seized a quick glance my way.

Aella leant into me. 'You should speak with him, there is something odd about this I think. After all it is a pretty dress Kate, are you sure you are not trying to catch someone's attention.'

'Aella! We are just friends.' Friends that I believed were both single enjoying each other's company and a mutual attraction. Now Sarah was on the scene I wasn't convinced we could still be friends. How would that work? The plan for our next adventure now truly out the window. I wasn't sure I wanted anything to do with the man. Aella gave one of her knowing smiles, walking swiftly away from me.

Nico's face surfaced in my mind in a flash and I closed my eyes, a powerful image of the kiss presented itself. I had a sudden urge to see him, especially as George had a wife! I still couldn't believe what had unfolded and decided to get another drink to take my mind off George, hoping it would put me in a better mood and then search for Jack.

Jack had done a disappearing act and so had

Millie, it hadn't taken him long to claim his next victim, but I guess he was a free agent. On this island anyway.

Before long I found myself chatting to one of Stavros's sisters. Unlike Jack and me, there was no mistaking the resemblance to her brother. Such a funny lady, her laughter loud and quite infectious, telling me all about Stavros when he was a boy and the mischief he got up to. Their parents apparently clueless to his antics and how she had to make up quite a few tales to cover for him. Our chat a welcomed distraction until I spotted George making his way over to us. Stavros's sister moved on when she saw him approaching and winked at me. What had Aella told her?

'Hello stranger,' George said.

The muscles in my neck and shoulders tensed. I didn't reply and thought what an odd thing for him to say. What did he think I was going to do? Pounce on him when he arrived to the party as he stood beside his wife.

'I've been wanting to talk to you since I arrived.' Now he wanted to talk because it was convenient for him.

'Is that so.' My response cool in comparison to previous times. George shuffled to my side.

'You look lovely tonight,' he said. I couldn't quite believe he was saying this to me when there was a much bigger issue that he wasn't apologising for.

I turned to face him ready to vent my anger but got distracted, the top two buttons of George's brilliant white shirt were undone, not too much yet enough. What I really wanted to tell him was how handsome he looked and how fabulous he smelt. He was a married man, clearly I couldn't say what I was thinking and waited for his explanation.

George looked in Sarah's direction and took a large measure of his red wine. I stood waiting for him to say something. His body motionless.

'Let's talk later, I think we are about to be summoned.' And he left me hanging as he walked away.

It was my turn to stand motionless, not understanding what just occurred. George sounded abrupt and I felt even more dejected. I contemplated leaving.

Giggling laughter from the side of the house made me turn my head, Jack and Millie came into view with beaming smiles on their faces.

'There you are, we are about to eat.'

'Yes, here we are dear sister.' Jack placed his arm around my shoulder and Millie gave a sheepish smile before setting off to find her parents.

Seats filled quickly and I saw Aella pointing to

where we were seated. George and his family took the seats opposite us on the large round table. I was flabbergasted Aella had done that, was she purposely trying to cause a reaction from me? Well I would rise above the situation I'd been forced into. George promised to talk to me later about what had been going on and I hoped he would keep his word. I deserved an explanation. I demanded an explanation!

I attempted to enjoy the food and chatted to Jack, so that he kept his eyes off Millie.

'What's this?' Jack asked, then swallowed his food.

'Calamari.'

'Quite delicious, who would have thought it could taste this good.'

I pushed my food around the plate, managing a couple of mouthfuls.

'Enjoying yourself?'

'Yep. There is a lot to take in, especially the views,' he said with a contented smirk on his face. Jack lifted his wine glass. 'To us.'

I lifted my glass to his. 'Yamas.'

'Yamas,' he said.

I could sense George looking my way and I caught his stare for mere seconds before turning to speak with the man sat on my other side. Our conversation focussed on the delicious food and then him asking how I enjoyed living on the island. I attempted the odd Greek word during our chat.

The meal appeared to be dragging on and at one point I caught Sarah observing Jack as he focussed in on Millie. A small frown formed between Sarah's perfectly plucked eyebrows no doubt trying to work out if Jack's intentions were good. As if she sensed I studied her, our eyes met and I forced a smile then looked away, at the same time Aella stood. Aella announced the time had come to present Stavros with his surprise.

A cake arrived. But not just any cake, this thing was huge, it had three tiers and neatly covered in white icing, edged with swirling gold piping. It took two people to carry the cake and the base it was mounted upon. The numerous candles were lit. Led by Aella and Stephon, standing on his chair, we all stood and sang happy birthday to Stavros in Greek obviously, which I am ashamed to say I mimed to and Jack sang in English. We raised our glasses and toasted to Stavros's good health with an ouzo as he remained seated in his chair.

Guests started to move away from their tables and a four piece band appeared playing Greek music. Jack jumped to his feet with urgency, grabbed his drink and winked at me, off to accost Millie. She was cute, in fact they did look good together. I hoped he was gentle with her feelings, he didn't have a great track record.

Glancing down at my empty glass, I poured more red wine from the bottle in front of me. I avoided making eye contact with either George or Sarah. I took a small sip, I needed to slow the pace of my drinking.

I felt two firm hands on my shoulders, Stavros had approached and insisted I dance with him. We joined a large circle already formed. My shoulder intertwined with Stavros on the left and his sister on the right, kicking my legs in a random fashion until I managed to get in time. The band stopped and I grabbed my breath, realising my fitness wasn't the best. The music began again and while we danced I noticed Sarah talking to one of Stavros's colleagues. George had disappeared.

I registered that this was my chance to talk with George, but needed an excuse to escape from Stavros. I questioned whether this was the right time and place to talk to George and if there was any point at all. Aella came up behind me.

'Now is your chance, George is waiting for you.' Aella whispered into my ear and pointed discreetly to the bottom of the garden. How was Aella so sure I wanted to talk to him?

Aella slid into my position and I took a quick glance across to where Sarah stood. Satisfied to see she still chatted away, drink in hand, seemingly enjoying the attention as more people gathered around her.

Making my way between the large trees, a strong scent of pine hit my senses. The ground became more uneven as I placed one foot in front of the other and grabbed hold of branches to steady my walk.

I found him staring out towards the sea. He had his back to me and I coughed loud enough for him to know I'd arrived. George turned towards me. No light where he stood only the brightness of a full moon shining above us in the clear night sky. The wine I had steadily drank had taken effect and I was trying to keep my feet steady waiting for George to speak.

Hands in his pockets. 'I don't know where to start. I didn't know Millie was arriving, not yet anyway and I was even more surprised to find Sarah standing next to her.'

I stayed silent.

'Sarah and I are no longer together, or so I thought.' He paused. 'I'd signed the bloody divorce papers and believed she had to. Now she has turned up and says she wants me to take her back, wants to move out here permanently.' A heavy sigh left his lips.

George turned his body towards the sea again,

as if what he told me embarrassed him.

He continued, 'Before she came out here there was absolutely no way on earth I would take her back, but she is grinding me down slowly. This is what she does.' He shook his head from side to side. 'Saying I am the only man she has ever truly loved, turning on the water works.'

Why wasn't George giving Sarah another chance? From what I'd witnessed you could tell how much she still cared for him.

'Do you still love her?' I piped up.

George turned to face me. 'I will always have feelings for the woman, she's the mother of our child. I thought she loved me until...'

'Perhaps she still does.' I couldn't believe I was sympathetic towards Sarah after all she was my rival.

'She's had her chances over the years, first ...' George stopped mid-sentence again. 'Anyway I've changed and moved my life on,' he stated.

I wasn't ready to forgive George just yet, how could I be confident that what he was telling me was true. If Sarah wasn't what he wanted, why hadn't he told her to leave immediately?

Finding the courage to say what dwelled on my mind. 'Does that include being dishonest to me?' Dishonest probably too strong a word, we hadn't kissed yet, although I believed it to be a real possibility for when we next met.

He didn't reply and looked down to the floor. I'd had enough and turned to head back to the house, this wasn't a game to me.

'Wait.' George pulled me towards him and kissed me firmly on the lips. He pulled his mouth away for a second, 'I'm falling for you.' And then he kissed me passionately and I didn't hold back, my hands found their way to the back of his neck as I melted into the warmth of his mouth. His hands caressing my hips as we gave in to each other.

'Here you two are.'

We both froze. Our bodies locked. How long had Aella been standing there?

We parted and turned towards her.

'You found each other, good. Sarah has been asking where you are George, you had better get back before she gets suspicious.'

As if Aella had given George a military order he glanced my way before he disappeared through the trees. I have to say I quite surprised myself but relieved the steam pressure had been released within me. To say I was disappointed to see Aella an understatement.

'So what has been happening here Kate, you can tell your good friend Aella all about it.' She linked her arm underneath mine.

'I like him Aella, but it's complicated,' was all I'd commit. Sensing she wasn't thrilled with my brief response by her silence, we made our way back to the celebration. I held firm with my silence, a smug smile on my face.

As we stepped closer, Jack stood amongst a modest gathering, appearing to hold court. Millie was not part of Jack's audience, perhaps he had got bored of her already were my initial thoughts. Aella and I watched on while my brother entertained his admirers. Stavros snuck up behind me.

'Here she is, come back to dance with Stavros.' How could I refuse the birthday boy.

I spotted George standing under one of the large lit trees watching us. Stavros held out his hands and I placed mine in his, giving him my attention. I tried to enjoy the moment with Stavros but it was a challenge, I really wanted to be with George. It should have been us dancing together.

'Enjoying yourself?' Stavros asked. I glanced over to where George was standing and he had disappeared.

About to answer Stavros when he said, 'Excuse me.' He released my hands.

Stavros walked towards a small crowd. I made my way forward concerned someone had taken ill.

As I got closer, George lifted Sarah up from the ground. She was crying as he managed to get her to her unsteady feet. Sarah appeared very drunk, the scene humiliating for George.

Chapter 21

We galloped along the sand close to the water's edge. I held on tightly to my gallant rider, who rode the black stallion hard. The horse came to a halt, the rider dismounted, his firm hands on my waist and he lifted me down. We collapsed onto the golden sand, exhausted from our exhilarating ride. As I lay back I turned to feast on the man who lay close to me. He leaned towards me, brushing my wind swept hair gently from my face. Who was he? I couldn't see his face. And then his lips were upon mine.

My body jolted upright, my mouth dry as I took in the familiar sights around me. What was the significance of that dream I wondered? I lay back and looked up at the ceiling and noticed a crack I'd never spotted before. I traced the line from one side of the room to the other until it came to a stop and then reflected on the last couple of days.

What's that saying about buses? I had three men in my life now who occupied my thoughts, and it would appear not only during the day but maybe a hidden message in my sleep.

George had made his feelings obvious for me at the party. I traced the outline of my lips, wondering how long our interlude would have gone on for if Aella hadn't arrived. In fact I had no idea how long she'd been standing there. I'm certain I wouldn't have responded so forwardly if I hadn't drank so much wine.

An image of us sharing that hot kiss under the moonlit sky and a deep sigh left my lips. I wondered if George was thinking of it too. Or the moment lost when he took Sarah back to his house. I knew I had no grounds to doubt how George felt about me, but had a sneaking suspicion Sarah would continue to try and wear George down.

And then there was my visit to Nico's house, the previous day. That sweet innocent kiss and on the lips. If I hadn't knocked on his door and been so pushy with my questions how long would it have taken him to kiss me? If at all.

And Jack, my brother, staying whilst conducting these liaisons. Wasn't I supposed to be the more sensible out of the two siblings? Maybe it was just as well he was visiting, allowing me to take my mind off both George and Nico or that was what

I sought to convince myself. Jack only had a few more days left with me, I guessed, and I wasn't sure I was ready for him to leave yet. Although, he still hadn't confirmed when he was returning back to England. Another deep sigh left my lips and I rolled onto my side.

He is wearing one of his crazy loud shirts, a bottle of beer in his hand and an irresistible smile that lit up my world. I am wearing a garish pink top, my hair scooped up on top of my head, displaying wooden hooped earrings. In my hand a tall cocktail of some description, possibly a Singapore Sling. We look so young sat in the Kalymnos bar. The photograph always bringing a smile to my face as I recalled that fateful night when we came across the 'cave' bar.

My finger stroked the glass, circling his smiling face.

'What do you make of all this?'

Slowly I rolled out of bed.

I registered it was Monday and if Jack hadn't been staying and I hadn't drank so much wine I'd be writing by now. I didn't have the energy. Jack was sparked out when I checked in on him, fully clothed, face buried in the pillow, his long legs dangling over the end of the bed.

I skipped breakfast and decided I quite fancied a swim. This was most unlike me, I had only been swimming twice since I'd lived on the island. The first time, a day in February and the sun shone brightly, but not for long before it started to rain. The second time, actually I don't recall there being a second time.

I had a swimming costume somewhere and eventually found it hidden in the back of a drawer. As I wriggled into the costume, it felt snugger than the last time I'd worn it. I can't remember where I bought it from, or why I had chosen blue with faded horizontal pink stripes printed on it. No doubt it would have been more suited to someone a lot younger than me such as Millie for instance.

I grabbed a towel and headed out hoping the sea water would help soothe my headache and calm my confused mind.

I stood at the water's edge, breathing in and out, in and out and exercised my arms in a large circular motion. I ventured into the sea cautiously, one foot at a time and then took the plunge in.

After the initial shock from the coolness of the water my body quickly adjusted. It did that the sea, tricked you into thinking it were warmer than it actually was, just because it was being bathed in sunshine. Effectively I had my own private beach and swimming area, not many people could say that.

I lay back and closed my eyes and floated in the gentle swaying motion. The sea engulfed my loose hair, my body weightless. My mind decluttering of any thoughts, as my hands moved gently back and forth keeping me afloat. Why hadn't I done this more often? After all I had no spectators.

I turned my head and glanced towards the shore. I saw his jet black hair first. He was sitting on a large rock under a tree. I couldn't quite work out what he was wearing, it obviously wasn't his usual attire. He saw that I had spotted him and waved. I wasn't sure I was ready to see him. I quickly realised I definitely wasn't ready to see him.

Swimming quickly to the shore, I picked up my towel and speedily wrapped it around me tightly. He had started to make his way towards me. I couldn't compute what I was seeing, he wore dark blue shorts and a white short sleeved shirt. On anybody else would have looked perfectly normal, and I couldn't hide my amusement at the sight of Nico in his casual wear. I began to laugh, the kiss he had planted seemingly disappeared.

'And what is so amusing?' Nico asked as he approached.

'You are, I have never seen you like this.'

'It is my day off,' he said and continued, 'how you can say that to me when you are standing wrapped in a towel.' He had a point, my hair dripping wet, hanging across my shoulders like wet seaweed no doubt.

His day off? I didn't think priests had a day off, then again it was a profession like anything else. Why hadn't he mentioned this before? What did he do on his days off? Did he have a hobby? This was something I wanted to probe into further.

'Good point, I need to change. I can make tea if you like?'

'Yes, I would like that.' The only slightly annoying trait about Nico, you never knew if he truly liked anything, because the tone in his voice never changed. However that was the only criticism I found about him.

We headed back to my house neither of us speaking, unusual for us, probably more so for me. The silence causing an unnatural divide as the kiss came into my thoughts again. Jack also popped into my thoughts and although it was now past midmorning I hoped he wasn't awake to see me walking beside Nico. Both of us being unusually attired.

'Why don't you wait for me here Nico while I change.' I steered him to our usual spot at the table in my garden.

Tip toeing around, deciding to leave my shower as the bathroom was next to Jack's room, I quickly dressed into shorts and a t-shirt. I scooped my damp hair up and looped the band around a few times.

My pulse raced, flying down the stairs to the kitchen. I made tea and grabbed a few pieces of fruit which I placed on a tray. The decorative tray covered in wild flowers and butterflies, one of the few sentimental items I brought with me and a gift from my mother-in-law. The sight of the tray stirring guilt in me, I had not spoken to Anne for quite some time. I made a mental note to call her and made my way out into the garden.

'Here we are, I haven't eaten breakfast yet, help yourself.'

'Let me.' Nico poured the tea. He appeared at ease and his casual clothes somehow softened the importance of his calling in life.

I picked up a nectarine and started munching hoping I didn't have to speak first, wishing I'd pretended I hadn't seen him and turned to swim in the opposite direction.

'How was the party for your friend Stavros?' Nico asked as he seated. Without his priest garments he looked like any other man. No he didn't, he was way more attractive than any other man. Apart from George of course. I tried not to stare at his bare legs just visible under the table, but it was highly tempting.

I placed the stone of the fruit on the tray, wishing I had grabbed a handful of tissue to place it in. 'Very good, we had a lovely time.'

'We?'

'Yes, me and Jack.' My night certainly ended on a positive note as George's face came to mind. My finger traced the outline of my lips once again. Nico watched me and I managed a brief smile.

A small bird appeared with a bright orange beak perching itself on one of the large pots, no doubt in search for easy food. Undeterred by our presence it sat and prodded at its feathers, an uninvited visitor to our private party. I felt the urge to shoo it away.

Nico cleared his throat and I averted my gaze back to him.

'Kate. I should not have kissed you like that.'

A piercing noise drew my eyes back to our feathered eavesdropper. Why was it hanging around? An odd looking bird; eyes too big for its head.

Nico stood and I assumed he'd decided to leave, already. And then he took a couple of steps to face me. I looked up and felt his hands on the tops of my shoulders. He gently pulled me to my feet. His eyes intense and he kissed me. This time with more urgency and passion, my body experiencing an instant charge from the touch of his lips and a briskness from his unshaven face.

I pulled away first, my pulse speeding, quickly realising what just happened in daylight for everyone to witness. It was lucky this side of the house wasn't visible from the road.

'I think I am falling in love with you Kate,' Nico announced.

A gasp of air escaped from my lips, loud enough for him to hear. 'Really?' Probably not the response he hoped for. This scene moving at a faster pace than I was keeping up with. 'I mean are you certain?' That sounded even worse.

Nico released his hands from my shoulders. 'I hoped you may have feelings for me too?'

'Well of course I do.' My eyes drawn towards the ground unable to look at his face.

'But not quite the same?' Nico returned to his seat as did I.

I couldn't believe we were actually having this conversation even though I am ashamed to say I had played it out in my imagination before. I wasn't convinced I was in love with him. How could Nico make such a statement?

'I didn't think you were allowed to have a relationship,' I eventually said.

'It is complicated yes, but not unachievable.'

'I thought I heard voices out ...' Jack stopped mid-sentence.

We both looked towards him, was the guilt written all over our faces? He clearly wasn't expecting to see Nico and especially dressed in his casual clothes.

'Day off for you is it Nico?' Jack asked and proceeded to fold his arms, leaning against the door frame.

'Yes,' Nico replied. It felt to me a repeat of the last time they met, and I wasn't much help in my confused state.

Thankfully, Nico was a good reader of situations. 'I should be on my way, perhaps we can talk later Kate?'

'Yes okay,' I responded automatically.

Nico left and I watched him stride away. My pulse still quicker than normal.

'Earth to Kate, come in Kate.'

I took in a deep breath and exhaled before I turned back to face my brother. 'Jack, did you have a nice lie in?' My attempt at changing the subject.

'What was that all about?' It didn't work. Jack sounded just like dad.

'Nico popped by on his day off,' I replied matter of fact.

'Is that so. And you expect me to believe that?'

I thought I had been discreet about my feelings towards Nico. What were my feelings towards Nico? There was no time to analyse them at that precise moment. What if Jack had appeared minutes earlier?

'Don't be silly, he was getting my advice about something.'

'Really. Does George know you have another admirer?'

'What has George got to do with anything?' Jack didn't respond. I hadn't told him what happened at Stavros's party. 'I think George has other things on his mind at the moment, don't you,' I said raising my eyebrows.

I picked up the untouched tea and placed it on the tray. 'Out of my way Jack.' He stepped aside and I successfully managed to put an end to that conversation. Jack could be exceedingly persistent when he wanted to be, a family trait and I didn't want him to catch me out in what was clearly becoming a complicated situation.

Chapter 22

I decided to take that shower. The lukewarm water sprinkled over me; in no way like the power shower I had back in England. I closed my eyes and thought back to the passionate kiss with Nico. Totally unexpected. I wondered if he could taste the residue of salt water on my lips. I fantasised that if Jack hadn't been staying what might have happened next. I imagined Nico in the shower with me, our bodies tantalising each other and dared my imagination further, him taking me to my bedroom to make love to me. This replaced with another image that I led Nico to my bedroom and he made love to me and then we took a shower together.

I heard Jack's voice outside the bathroom door, halting my fantasies. Which is exactly what they were.

I turned off the shower.

'I said, I'm going out,' Jack said.

'Okay.'

Getting out of the shower I stood on the plastic cover and cursed. Jack's electric razor had been left in a hurry its guard fallen to the floor. Short haired fuzz lined the sink basin and the toilet seat was in the upright position, classic signs I was sharing a house with the opposite sex once again. I tutted as I dried myself and wandered into my bedroom.

I perched on the edge of my bed, wondering how I found myself in this situation. What was I going to do? I needed to talk to George, but recognised that would be difficult with Sarah and Millie staying. I also needed to talk to Nico too.

Wandering down to the kitchen, wrapped in my towel I made a pot of coffee, dwelling on what my next steps should be.

Jack had left me a note on the kitchen table.

I'M TAKING MILLIE OUT FOR SOME SIGHTSEEING, DON'T WAIT UP! Xx

Made me smile, he was determined to have fun while he was here. He had in all probability seen more of the island compared to the whole time I had lived here. How shameful. I didn't however feel there was a need to write in capital letters, my eye sight wasn't failing yet.

Jack's note confirmed two people were out of the way. How to meet George without Sarah? I suspected she wouldn't want to be apart from George for long if she was trying to win him back. Especially as in her eyes, they were still married. Aella of course, she would help. I called her number but she didn't answer, I tried again not wanting to leave a message. She answered the second time.

'Aella, it's me. Can you help me out with a favour?' Jumping straight in with my question.

'Yes, what is it?'

'Could you invite Sarah out for coffee or over to your place so that I can speak to George?'

'Yes just a moment, let me find the number.' What was Aella talking about and then she spoke again, her voice quieter, 'She is already here.' That was a surprise.

'Really, why?' Even though I had suggested Aella invite Sarah over I wasn't sure I was now happy with them meeting up. After all, Aella was my friend.

'George dropped Sarah here ten minutes ago, said he had a work issue. I think he is on his way over to you.'

'Oh. How do you know?'

'Just a guess. Perhaps you should get ready for

him.' I heard a cheekiness to her tone.

'Aella!'

My heart started pounding.

George arrived five minutes after finishing my brief conversation with Aella. My hair still damp from the shower, I hadn't even put a brush through it and I'd thrown on an old shirt, the first thing I put my hands on which barely covered my bottom. I wasn't dressed for receiving visitors but didn't have time to change.

George knocked and I hadn't had time to prepare myself mentally or physically for his visit. I took in a deep breath and smoothed my fingers over my hair. 'It's open.'

He stepped inside and without turning he closed the door behind him and advanced towards me. George looked hot, his shirt sleeves rolled back revealing his tanned arms.

'Coffee? It's not long made,' I asked needing a distraction.

'Sure,' George replied, his voice unreadable. This only the second time he had been inside my house.

I took a quick glance at my empty vase remembering the red carnations as George took a seat at the kitchen table. He seemed oblivious to my second hand furniture, if he was shocked by my simple surroundings he didn't show it. If I'd known I would be having so many visitors it may have spurred me into action with some decorating.

I placed a cup in front of him, sensing his eyes on me as I poured his steaming coffee. I took my seat, tugging my shirt beneath me, conscious of my partially dressed state.

His eyes were fixed on mine when I looked up at his face. I wasn't sure whether to start the conversation but my mind had gone blank and I gave out a loud exhale of breath.

George cleared his throat. 'I meant what I said to you last night.'

I picked up my coffee and blew over the hot liquid and then took a sip, relieved he hadn't changed his mind about me. Unable to respond straight away, I watched as his hand moved to his cup and rested there.

I found the courage to look at him hoping he would say more and I didn't have to wait long.

'It's over between me and Sarah,' he said with assertion.

'Really?'

'Yes,' he said with conviction. His hands rested on the table clasped firmly together. 'And.' He paused. 'I have feelings for you.'

The vibration of my breathing now loud in my ears.

'You do?' I don't know why I needed for him to confirm this again. And he had already told me how he felt at the party.

George smiled. 'Yes I do.'

Unable to contain the smile I gave back and feeling brave I asked, 'Okay, what does that mean?'

'I'd like to see you, properly.'

I wanted to ask what Sarah's plans were. Had George asked her to leave, had he told her they were truly over? Then as if he were reading my mind.

'I've asked Sarah to leave.' His eyes moved to survey the contents of his cup. 'She suspects I have met someone else.' He looked up, his eyes meeting mine again, his lips narrowing. 'It wasn't a pleasant scene when I told her to go back to England.' George didn't elaborate any further.

'How do you feel?' he asked lifting his cup to take his first drink.

How did I feel? I was feeling buzzy that George seemed genuinely interested in me, unfortunately a flash back appeared in my mind to when Nico kissed me earlier. It dawned on me that had Nico not left, George would have come to the house and seen us glued at the lips. I envisaged that would have been a dramatic scene. I needed time to answer his question but couldn't see how to delay my answer with George sitting in front of me. It was my move in the chess game.

'This is all moving a bit fast, don't you think?' Maybe it wasn't for him, but I didn't think I could handle much more emotion in one day and now questioning why I felt the urgency to see him so soon. And yet he had turned up unannounced.

George took another drink from his cup. I suspected I had said the wrong thing.

'Are you sure Sarah is leaving?' Not totally convinced she would just give up on the love of her life. I certainly wouldn't. My sensible head told me I didn't need to be a distraction for George until Sarah had left. I didn't want to be caught up in a love triangle. Then it occurred to me I was in one of my own with George and Nico. I had absolutely no experience of the predicament I found myself in. In the past, before I met Paul, one relationship at a time was good enough for me and to be honest there weren't that many. I didn't want to lose my friendship with George or Nico and unsure what either was developing into.

At that moment George lent across the table and placed his hand on mine. I let it rest there enjoying the warmth and tingling sensation floating up my arm and then my whole body met with a flow of heat. I thought of something to say that would give George reassurance before my body erupted.

'I do have feelings for you George.' There, I said what was truly on my mind. But what about Sarah, until she left I knew I couldn't see George again.

'I will talk to her again and make certain she is in no doubt about leaving,' he replied straight away. 'Even if I have to book her plane ticket myself.' He sounded serious.

He moved his hand slowly from mine and stood. I didn't want him to go. He stepped closer and looked at me through his stunning green eyes, they were mesmerising and I braced myself for what would happen next.

He leant down towards me and I closed my eyes, his lips on mine for what felt like seconds and then he pulled away.

'I need to go,' he said, his voice gentle.

Another shared glance and he walked away to leave. He stopped at the door and turned. For a moment he stood motionless, his lips parted and then changing his mind they quickly closed. He left and I was wishing he hadn't.

Chapter 23

After George departed, I decided I must talk to Nico knowing it was absurd we could be anything more than friends. I shook my head in disbelief.

It was midafternoon by the time I dressed in respectful clothes. Jack's note said don't wait up, I concluded he would be quite some time having fun with Millie somewhere. I assumed George was okay with Millie and Jack, he hadn't mentioned anything to me earlier but I guess he had his own scenario to deal with. As indeed I now had too.

I tied my hair back and a final glance in the mirror to ensure I looked presentable, not knowing how my conversation with Nico would play out when I arrived at his house. I just hoped he would be there. I needed to take control of this ridiculous situation we had gotten into.

And then a knock at the door.

'Really?' I said out loud, not expecting anyone else. I looked out of my bedroom window to find a taxi. I made my way downstairs.

I couldn't hide the shock of seeing Sarah in my doorway.

'Can I come in?' Her body language unreadable.

'Sure.' What else could I say.

Firstly how did she know where I lived and secondly how did she travel from Aella's so quickly. An image of Sarah on a broomstick sprang into my mind.

'So, this is what he wants?' she said with a steeliness. A tone I'd not heard before.

'Sorry?'

She didn't turn to face me. 'I'm not stupid. I see the way he looks at you.' I didn't respond as I took in her immaculate state. A new look today, dressed in an embroidered white Caftan, gold gladiator sandals, teamed with a tan leather bag as if she were holidaying in St Tropez. My white cotton dress in competition, we had somehow managed to wear the same colour yet again.

I remained silent as she looked disapprovingly at my surroundings. I didn't offer her a drink or ask her to sit down. I didn't know what agenda she had come with.

She turned to face me. 'Nothing to say?'

My shoulders lifted in response.

'I find that surprising, I thought you writers were full of words,' she snapped.

I plucked up the courage. 'What has George told you exactly?'

'Nothing. He doesn't have to.' She looked towards the window and I followed her gaze as she appeared to fix on Paul's ashes. It wasn't a good spot for him, too much emotion being unleashed.

Sarah continued, 'You're not the first you know and certainly won't be the last. Although, his normal type is brunettes.' That blow caught me straight between the eyes and she knew it. Astounded by what she had said and not wanting to believe there could be any truth in her statement. George still hadn't told me what had happened between them. I didn't respond. If she had come here for some kind of fight I wasn't giving her one.

'I've seen enough,' she said and if looks could kill she forced a smirk and turned to leave, the taxi's engine still purring outside.

She came to wound me and put doubt in my mind. That she did without prolonging her visit.

As I approached his house, an old man and his small black dog were hovering in front of Nico's front door. I crossed to the other side of the street avoiding them, slowing down my pace. They weren't in a hurry.

I suddenly had second thoughts and continued walking until I came to another street, the adrenalin now working overdrive in my body. This whole situation I found myself in seemed crazy. Paul's face filled my mind and I became cross that he had left me to deal with a scenario that wasn't in our plan. Yes people fell out of love and parted, but that wasn't us, life wasn't fair. Was he looking down on me wondering what I had gotten myself into?

I came to a halt, shook my head from side to side and told myself I had come this far, now or never, best to get it over with and find out what was going on in Nico's mind. And more importantly tell him what was in mine.

I walked back along his street, glancing around to make certain there were no prying eyes. I stood before his door and paused, then knocked lightly on his door, just the once thinking if he didn't answer at least I could say I'd tried when questioned later.

I started to walk away not giving him enough time to answer, my arms relaxing into my sides.

'Kate.'

My left hand reached up to my heart as I took in a sharp intake of breath and I turned back towards him. I felt lightheaded. My expression must have changed, Nico picked up on this and helped me into his house.

He seated me on the small green sofa and proceeded to get me a glass of water.

'Here, drink this,' he said.

Shakily I lifted the glass to my lips and sipped on the welcomed cold drink.

'Better?'

'Yes.' I took another sip. 'I think it is too hot for me today,' I said breathlessly.

He sat beside me. 'Too hot you say.' Nico's attempt to make light of my episode. If only he knew how attractive he was. In fact, I recall Aella commenting on how handsome Nico was and what a waste he had devoted himself to God. She told me the female congregation numbers increased when he arrived.

Finding my voice. 'You said you wanted to talk, I assumed you meant today.'

'Yes, I hoped you would come. Does Jack know where you are?' I thought it strange he would ask if I needed my brother's permission.

'He has taken Millie out for the day. George's daughter.' My teeth clenched saying his name that I had let him reel me in again, to be then told I wasn't the first woman he had strayed with.

'We have some time together,' he said.

I looked at him quizzically and carried on drinking the rest of my water until I finished the last drop.

'Shall I get you more?' I shook my head to decline.

Nico took the glass from me and placed it back in the kitchen and promptly returned. His body came to a standstill in front of me and I lifted my gaze.

Nico looked serious, I had no hint of what he was thinking and then he held out his hand and I found myself placing mine in his. He gently pulled me to my feet and led me up the spiral staircase, my hand still in his.

Instead of going up to the next level and out onto the patio, he took a couple of steps to the right along a short corridor. He opened the dark wooden door and I followed him in.

Nico didn't speak as he led me towards his large bed, simply dressed; a golden throw over pure white sheets. He turned to face me releasing my hand and as I looked up his eyes were fixed intently and his pupils enlarged. I froze, my body unable to move from his stare.

He lent forward and kissed me gently on my forehead, the tip of my nose and across to my neck. Sensations awoken, buried for a long time. I stood rooted to the spot.

His eyes were on mine again and I felt his fingers on the small buttons at the front of my dress (I didn't consciously wear it and hadn't worn it since the Greek wedding and Nico's comment). My hands shot up and covered his and he moved both my hands back to my sides. My body pulsated with an overwhelming desire I felt inside.

The dress dropped to my feet and I gasped. Nico's hands moved to my shoulders and he gently turned me around. I closed my eyes, the only sound his heavy breathing and my heart quickened in response. His soft fingers now on my back and he released the hooks of my bra. Then warmth from his hands, the straps easing from my shoulders before falling to the floor. My eyes still closed, my breathing high in my chest, waiting for his next move.

Slowly I felt the last item sliding down my legs and then nothing. I opened my eyes and found Nico kneeling in front of me. He kissed me slowly in small steps from my navel up to my breasts and he kissed each of them gently.

'You are beautiful,' he said and then the fullness of his lips met with mine.

We lay in each other's arms, silent, enjoying the closeness of each other's bodies. I couldn't speak for him but I most certainly enjoyed his and not one thought for George crossed my mind.

I think it was getting on for early evening, though I couldn't be certain. The windows were dressed with heavy red curtains, partially closed, blocking out most of the light. Nico got up first and I admired the view of his naked body, it did not disappoint.

'Are you hungry?' he asked.

'Yes ravenous.' I hadn't eaten a thing since the nectarine during my first encounter with Nico that day. Probably explained my dizzy spell earlier and fuelled by the anxiety of meeting him of course.

'Help yourself to the shower, it is through there,' Nico said as he dressed, pointing to a curtain in the corner of the room. Then he left me alone in his bedroom.

I casually got up and my clothes lay on the floor. I scooped them up and placed them on his bed. I tried to remember when I had lay anywhere other than my own bed and of course I had not. Not in recent times and apart from when I'd fallen asleep on my sofa but that didn't count.

I took in my surroundings, the room was sparsely furnished and my eyes were drawn to a picture in a gold frame hanging on the wall. The oil painting, rich in colour of two small boats moored on the sand, its background water aqua blue. There was a signature in the right hand corner. Initial 'N' and I couldn't make the rest out. 'N' for Nicolaos perhaps, could this be his hobby?

I was still on a high from our lovemaking and couldn't quite lose the smirk fixated on my face as I pulled aside the curtain. I found a small bathroom: a shower cubicle, toilet and basin.

I picked up a couple of towels from a basket just inside and hung them on a large hook I found on the wall. I stepped into the shower and found soap in a beaker and what looked like shampoo for my hair. No conditioner, oh well he'd seen my hair in worse states in fact that same morning when exiting the sea. Little did I know when I was worrying about him seeing me in my costume I would be revealing all later the same day!

I lathered the soap, the one Nico used on his magnificent body. I lifted the soap to my nose and as I suspected unperfumed, yet still heightened my senses, alerting me to the natural scent of Nico. That would explain why he always smelt fresh, not scented. The shampoo had a citrus smell to it and I massaged the liquid into my hair. Cleanliness is next to godliness so they said.

That thought stopped me dead in my tracks.

Feeling sudden shame, the smirk wiped from my face. What had we done? Look what I had made Nico do. What was I thinking? I wasn't thinking. An image of George flew into my head. I closed my eyes, shaking my head, knowing I hadn't given him the chance to defend himself.

I hastily finished my shower, returned to Nico's bedroom and quickly dressed, my fingers fumbling on the buttons. I debated whether to leave straight away but didn't know how I'd explain myself to Nico. I recognised I needed to face up to what happened between us, I was a grown woman not some silly teenager.

I went up to the next level and glanced at the photographs, my eyes drawn to the female on her own and then out onto the patio area. There I found Nico, he had already put food and drink on the table for us to share.

'Enjoy, I will take my shower now,' he said flexing the muscles of his mouth into a generous grin.

I sat and glanced at the food in front of me but my stomach was churning. I started biting on my bottom lip, something I wasn't conscious of doing before. I wanted to flee before Nico returned.

No creaking stairs to contend with, only the sound of shower water running. I left his house, my hair still wet without as much as a goodbye to Nico. Like a villain leaving the crime scene. He didn't deserve this but I wasn't happy with the situation I had put myself or him in.

Chapter 24

It was starting to get dusky as I made my way back and I was desperate to return home to be in my safety zone. Unfortunately I had to pass by the church, but I kept my eyes firmly fixed on the road ahead of me. I assumed Jack would still be out with Millie therefore I would have some time to myself, but I wasn't sure that was what I wanted either. What did Nico make of my vanishing act? Was he experiencing any guilt about what had happened between us?

Relieved to be home, I poured a glass of water at least deciding I needed to keep my body hydrated if nothing else. Not surprisingly my appetitive completely disappeared. As I put the empty glass down on the worktop, my eyes glanced towards Paul's ashes. I looked away.

After pacing around the kitchen, lapping the

table several times, I sat and attempted to write a few words knowing there wasn't a chance I would get off to sleep easily. As much as I tried, when I peered at the screen in front of me I had only written one sentence. A stupid idea to try.

I walked out the door to escape a claustrophobic feeling I couldn't shake. The freshness of the air quickly filling my lungs, as if it were breathing life into me and I headed towards the darkness of the water. I stayed on the sand, looking out into blackness before me, I waited for an answer. Nothing.

I returned home and highlighted the sentence typed earlier, pressing the delete button just as the familiar sound of my front door closed. I glanced at the clock on my screen, 11pm. Jack I presumed, not expecting anyone else at that late hour. Blinking up in my dazed state I focussed on his face as he sat before me.

'Hello sis, hard at work?' If only he knew.

'Jack, did you have a nice day with Millie?'

'Yes I did, and of course Millie did because she got to spend it with me,' he said cockily. I wondered if Jack had ever been let down by a woman or he said the things he did to get a reaction from me.

'Of course she did. I assume you have eaten?'

'Yes, I had a bite at George's place; that is some house.' It certainly was, I couldn't argue with that. Though I doubted I would ever go there again.

'Did he drop you off?'

'He did.' Jack flicked his trainers off. I needed to have a word with Jack about that very annoying habit, I was aware I wasn't the tidiest of people but he left his trainers wherever they landed. However tonight was not the time to pick a battle.

'Oh, I didn't hear his car.'

'He dropped me off up the road, said he didn't want to wake you.'

My hands started shaking and my vision became blurred. I forced myself to my feet to pour another glass of water and then steadying my breathing to slow deliberate breaths.

'What have you been up to?' Jack asked unaware I was holding myself together.

'Just a bit of writing,' I managed to reply, my back still turned to him.

'You still haven't told me what it's about.'

Taking a few more sips and thankfully less shaky, I turned around to face Jack.

'You look worn out,' he said. 'I didn't think writing was so taxing.'

Nico's naked body sprang into my mind and I struck it from my thoughts forthwith.

'I think I will call it a night, I'm quite tired.' The thought of having a long conversation not what I needed.

I started up the stairs.

'Oh before you go to bed, I thought you would like to know Sarah is definitely leaving,' Jack informed me.

I nodded in recognition.

'Aren't you going to say anything?'

I raised my eyebrows in response. 'See you in the morning Jack.' I climbed my creaky stairs flopping onto the bed and emptied my lungs with the biggest breath I could muster. I came to the island to escape stresses and strains of modern day life. I'd found a place where I could write freely and take life at a pace most people would envy. I had a situation I couldn't have dreamed up and it had got a lot out of control and I didn't like it.

I rolled on my side and looked at his face. I turned the frame over and switched off the bedside light.

Chapter 25

I tossed and turned during the night, not a revelation considering the events I had encountered during the day. 6:30am - I placed the frame back to its upright position and took a shower to try and revive my exhausted body, in an attempt to get me back into a recognisable state. Breakfast and coffee, no writing, I didn't feel creative but a stroll down to the sea that would do it for me.

I moved around the house quietly ensuring I didn't wake Jack and left a note on the table for when he woke. Although I suspected I'd be back before he stirred. I had fallen into a habit of leaving notes for him when leaving the house. This reminding me: I did exactly the same with Paul. I grabbed my hat and made my way down to the water's edge.

The sea lapped gently around my feet, the sun's

rays warming my skin, transporting me to a safe relaxing space. Reminding why I came to live here and a sense of control again. Getting back into my old routine and not making any contact with either George or Nico they might get the message I required some much needed breathing space. In my mind standing in my favourite spot it appeared that simple. I wasn't sure if Nico would ever speak to me again, who could blame him. He had taken a brave step out of his comfort zone and for what price? But as much as I tried I couldn't just cast aside my feelings for Nico or could I? During the time I had got to know Nico, it was clear to me he took his role as a priest seriously, and consequently why I felt so guilty about what happened between us.

I sat on the sand. Sarah was leaving, as George said she would. George was waiting for my invitation to our next outing, I couldn't even contemplate that, without trying to find out if there could be any truth in what Sarah had told me. Then a flashback to our brunch, sitting not far from this very spot and a desire flooded me to have more of his time. Then flitting to Jack, he originally said he was only staying for a couple of weeks. I was no further forward understanding what his plans were. Although that the least of my concerns.

I stood and my thoughts moved on to Aella. I suspected I might get a call from her to meet for coffee in the next few days, certain she would want to be updated on what had been developing between me and George. Where to start with that? I needed to come up with a pretty good excuse to delay meeting up with her.

Reluctantly I headed back to the house assuming Jack would be stirring soon. I pottered around moving the few ornaments in my sitting area. I considered cleaning the windows next, the sunshine highlighting their neglected state. Then deciding this would take some rigour and therefore not a priority. I moved into the kitchen instead and filled the large jug with water and stepped outside to replenish my plants, still amazed they were alive. This not the best idea as they reminded me of Nico and what we did.

Jack stirred at 9am, his feet stomping down each step.

'What are your plans for today? I was hoping you would like to spend the day with your sister,' I said keenly.

'I've sort of made arrangements to meet Millie, sorry.'

'That's okay, I guess you would rather spend more time with her, she is much prettier and younger.' I tried to conceal the disappointment in my voice and decided to ask him outright about his plans for returning home.

'Jack, have you booked your flight back to England?' As I asked this, the idea of me taking the trip back with him sounded a good option, escaping the madness encasing me.

'No I haven't. To be honest, I wasn't sure how long I was going to be staying for.' Jack raised his hands up as if he were having a hallelujah moment. 'I know I'd said I was only staying for a couple of weeks, but now I'm here I'd quite like to stay longer if that's okay with you?'

'Oh, I see. This wouldn't have anything to do with Millie would it?'

'A little. Hey, where can you buy a snorkel around here?'

Shrugging my shoulders. 'A shop.'

'What about one of those scooter bike thingies you take on the water. Do you think Millie would be more interested in that?'

'I have no idea what they are called or where you can hire one. Trying to impress Millie are you, didn't think you needed to.'

'I don't, I want to show her there is more to me than just this.' Jack pointed to his face.

'Sounds like hard work to me.'

'You don't like any form of exercise.'

'That's not true.'

'Prove it,' Jack said mockingly.

'I'm getting a bicycle.' My tongue got the better of me, it wasn't an untruth I hadn't done anything about it yet.

'Is that so.' Jack raised his eyebrows, one visibly higher than the other. 'I need to get ready now, George said he would pick me up and drop us at the bus station. Have you seen my dark blue t-shirt anywhere?'

I shook my head. 'He's coming here?' Not expecting to see George so soon.

Jack cocked his head to one side and folded his arms in the process. 'Yes, is that a problem?'

I didn't reply because it absolutely was a problem.

I wasn't sure if George would knock on the door as his car pulled up outside. I stayed well away from view just in case he wanted to speak to me, my guilty conscience feeling like it might strangle me.

'See you later, don't wait up,' Jack said as he left through the door, one trainer on and the other still in his hand.

'Have fun.' I doubted he heard me, the door closing behind him. His scent of aftershave wafting towards me.

Jack's departure date was still unknown. I had naively assumed he had already booked his return flight at the same time as his departure, not for one second imagining he would stay for longer than two weeks. It was now becoming clear to me that he wasn't in a rush to return home. Maybe after another day out with Millie, Jack would have a clearer view what he wanted to do.

A panic started to rise inside of me and my breathing quickened, it occurred to me after George dropped them off he might head back here. As the tips of my fingers tapped against each other I came up with the notion of popping to the town. That a stupid plan, there was a chance I could bump into Nico as I passed the church. My next idea to call Aella to see if she were free, even though meeting up with her sooner than I wanted.

'Aella it's me, can I come over?'

'Sure, it would be great to have a catch up.' What she really meant by that was, she wanted an update on the latest gossip.

'Is Stavros at home?'

'No he is out working,' Aella replied. In one of his mysterious locations no doubt. 'Why?' she added.

'No reason.'

'I'll send someone to collect you,' she said.

Chapter 26

Aella was in the garden when I arrived. I found her sitting on a swinging chair beneath a large tree, gently rocking back and forth as if she didn't have a care in the world, unlike me. This a proper garden, the sort you might see in a magazine and rightly maintained with the help of her gardener of course. Perhaps she could lend him to me, there was no question I needed help. A statue would be going too far though for my small plot, maybe a modest water feature and a hammock would suffice.

'Here you are, come and sit beside me.' A vision of a lioness preparing for her kill came to mind as she patted the space beside her. I had no escape now.

Stephon played with a brightly coloured ball and waved to me as I approached. I wondered if all children were as content as him, not having had much experience with them myself, I had no idea. You hardly noticed he was around when I visited, no wonder Aella's life appeared so stress free.

When I saw Stephon he didn't make me regret we hadn't had children. I never experienced those feelings people get; maternal instincts or broodiness. Paul wasn't fussed about children either. 'If it happens, it happens,' he would say. We were so content with each other, nothing appeared to be missing.

Prepared for my visit, Aella picked up the steel pot with a long handle and poured two coffees from the table beside her. She passed one to me. Nothing to go with them unfortunately, as I craved for something sweet to boost my energy levels.

Aella was quick to start the conversation going even though I had asked to see her. 'Do you want to know what I learnt from Sarah?'

No, I didn't want to know what she had learnt from Sarah I already knew, but reluctantly played the game in case there was more detail; half wanting to know and half not.

'I am sure you are going to tell me Aella.'

'Sarah had an affair with one of George's best friends.'

'What? Sarah had an affair?' My voice bordering

on screeching. Stephon looked our way and I was ashamed at my outburst. He waved and kicked his ball, chasing after it.

'There's more.' Aella took a quick breath. 'George found them in bed together.' I didn't respond. Aella continued, 'Finding out your wife is having an affair is one thing Kate but seeing them in bed together must have been devastating.'

'How long had it been going on?' I was quick to ask.

'She said a few months, but I am not convinced she was being honest with me.'

'Did George throw her out?'

'No, he did not. Apparently he kept quite calm.' Aella drank from her cup, she had more to say.

'What happened next?' I asked.

'The affair ended and Sarah and George attempted to make a go of their marriage. But she said their relationship wasn't the same.' Aella's free arm shot up to the sky. 'Six months later she went back to this other man and after a time this man didn't want her.' Aella's arm returned to her side and she lowered her voice. 'That is why she turned to the drink. And now she is here.'

To doubt George and believe there may have been some truth in what Sarah had told me. To assume George the villain and falling into Nico's arms and bed. Then again George hadn't been forthcoming in what happened between him and Sarah, what was I supposed to think? I couldn't understand why George would be so understanding when he found out about the affair, he must have truly loved her. For her to turn up here, desperate to be with him again. I still wasn't totally convinced that giving Sarah another chance hadn't crossed George's mind.

Finally I spoke. 'Wow, she told you all this.' For Sarah to tell me one thing and then blurt out the truth to Aella. I decided not to tell Aella about Sarah's visit, there didn't seem a need.

'I am not stupid Kate, she wants me to feel sorry for her and to speak to George. She wants to live here.' Of course Sarah did.

'Are you going to talk to George?'

'No, I will not. You are my friend.' A smugness filled Aella's beautiful face as she sipped on her coffee. I was thankful Aella fought my corner.

I drank from my cup watching Stephon chase after his ball.

'How have you been?' she asked.

I turned my head to face Aella.

'You are looking pale, are you okay?' She seemed concerned maybe I didn't look too great.

'Just didn't sleep very well last night.'

'And why is this, is it because of George?'

George, Nico, the chaos surrounding me. 'I'm a bit behind with my writing.' I wasn't ready to let her know what had been happening yet or even at all. Unfortunately Aella wasn't a patient lady.

'No this is something more I think.'

I was reluctant to say more, never too sure about Aella's sense of confidentiality.

She returned her cup to the table and poured more coffee. Glancing down, my cup now empty too. I passed my cup over to her, although another injection of caffeine not the healthiest option for my nervous system.

Aella's intuition was too good when I didn't respond. 'There is something else you have not told me,' her voice softer.

I stared down into my lap watching the tips of my fingers as they tapped against each other.

Aella passed over my refilled cup. 'You need to relax, I will send over my Yoga instructor. He is superb and extremely handsome.'

That was the secret to her stunning figure. I had attempted Yoga, just the once, remembering how I was instructed to contort my body into positions I didn't know possible. At the end of the class we lay on purple coloured mats in the darkened room, my eyes closed and our instructor saying something about a bright white light entering my body. The experience so not me. I wondered if Stavros had been introduced to Aella's 'extremely handsome' instructor.

Unable to keep the lid on my emotions they got the better of me. 'I've done something stupid Aella.' I drank from my cup. Aella remained quiet.

'It involves another man.' Now she knew the truth.

'No, who?' I sensed Aella's eyes boring into me.

'It's complicated.'

'How?'

'It just is.' I regretted telling her and looked towards the house in a bid to start my escape.

'Is he married?'

I turned to face her. 'No he's not married.'

Aella put her cup back on the table and faced me. 'You slept with this man?'

'Yes.'

'I don't understand, I thought you liked George.'

'It wasn't planned.' A sudden thought crossed my mind that it may have been Nico's intention for us to sleep together, after the kiss we shared.

'Who is this person, tell me his name, I must

know him.' It felt like she was firing bullets at me.

'No Aella, I won't disclose his name. I have ended it, I am not going to see him again.' Satisfied I had answered assertively, then quickly realised I hadn't actually ended anything and had no way of knowing when I would see Nico again.

Aella didn't respond straight away, most unlike the 'Amazon Warrior'. I think she was genuinely astonished by my announcement. It felt shocking saying it. And I guess she was amazed why I hadn't mentioned this mystery man before. Aella probably judged me not capable of having a fling.

An unusual silence wedged between us. I had nothing to add.

'How are you going to avoid this man, I assume he lives locally?' Aella asked, not put off by my previous response. I hadn't got around to thinking about that and it was a valid point.

'I'll think of something, I'll lie low for a couple of days.'

Aella's shoulders raised upwards. 'Lie low, what does this mean?'

'I will avoid him.' Deep down I acknowledged I would have to see Nico face to face, sooner rather than later. I was praying it would be later.

I stood from the swinging chair, deciding it was

for the best to leave and return back to my house. Aella insisted on taking me back herself, but first I had to wait for her to get changed into something more fitting for the act of driving.

I waited for her inside the house, glancing at my watch, wondering how long it took her to change. She returned five minutes later, her sun dress replaced with slim fitting red trousers, a long sleeved pink shirt with laced cuffs resting just above her knuckles. On her feet she wore white trainers, the first time I had witnessed such a sight. She was ready for the task ahead of her, I wasn't aware she could drive.

Stephon appeared excited to climb into the back seat. I turned to face him and watched Aella struggle as she strapped him in. She spoke assertively in Greek to her son and he quietened. I suspected it was something like, 'Stephon sit still, or I will leave you here on your own.'

Aella stalled the car twice before we eventually got going. It showed that she didn't get behind a wheel too often, staying in the same gear for most of our journey. Even so, I was glad of the ride back rather than a very long walk back in the heat, therefore I kept quiet and surprisingly so did Aella.

Aella saw him first. 'Oh look you have a visitor.'

He must have just knocked and turning to leave when he saw the car approaching.

I scratched the back of my neck. 'Would you like to come in for a while?' I asked Aella.

'No I must get back, anyway the priest is waiting for you,' she replied.

Aella didn't show any facial signs she suspected anything, why would she. I was thankful Nico hadn't turned up in his casual clothes because I judged she would have been suspicious of that. Then an almighty eruption would have occurred. Reluctantly I stepped out of her car.

Aella drove off on the wrong side of the road, waving an arm in the air. I envied her attitude to life sometimes and especially this day.

Chapter 27

I walked slowly to my door and met Nico's eyes. His expression unreadable.

'Hi, want to come inside?'

He nodded. The dreaded moment had arrived and it was too soon. I felt nauseous all of a sudden.

Nico followed me through my door and I registered it was the first time he had set foot in my house. We always had our cosy chats at the table in my garden. It seemed more appropriate to take our business inside away from potential prying eyes. I sensed our conversation was going to feel uncomfortable, and relieved knowing Jack would be out all day with Millie to allow us privacy.

'Tea?' He nodded and took Jack's usual seat.

I picked up the kettle and my hand began to shake, hoping he hadn't noticed as I performed the simple task. Unsure who should speak first, I took my time making the tea as he appeared in no rush to speak and neither was I. Wishing I'd stayed at Aella's longer.

I placed the mismatched cups on the table and poured. My hand had steadied but I was conscious he watched me intently. I felt like a child fearing they were going to be told off, the scene giving me a flashback to encounters with my parents.

He spoke first, no emotion. 'Why did you leave without saying goodbye?' The obvious question to start with.

I looked out of the window, hoping it would give me an appropriate answer but there was no point hiding what I believed inside.

'I felt ashamed of what I had done, what we had done.'

He fired back straight away. 'I am not ashamed of what happened between us.'

I turned my gaze back towards him and sat in my chair. 'How can you say that, you are a priest.' That hit the mark, he didn't reply and I looked away, my eyes focussing on my wedding band. It felt like we were a couple having our first serious argument.

'You have stirred a passion within me I believed had died,' he said, his voice softer. My body froze, unable to look at him. 'The times we have spent getting to know each other has made me realise how much I care for you, even though I may not show my feelings.' I still couldn't look his way. 'I would give it all up for you.'

A surge of waves hit me. My mind and body unprepared. That this conversation was actually happening. The very notion we could be together. When we slept together I didn't think about what would happen next, I was caught up in the moment. It certainly didn't occur to me I had a future with Nico. Could it be that easy, us being together? What would people say? Surely we couldn't stay on Kalymnos? My mind now turning resembling a hamster wheel and I needed for it to stop.

I met with his eyes. 'I can't ask you to do that Nico,' I replied with assertion.

He stood and slowly moved to stand facing the window. Clothed as a priest, serious Nico and not the Greek man I became intimate with the day before. His silent towering frame inches from Paul's ashes, yet I doubted he registered they were there. My fingers on my right hand now fiddling with the ring on my left finger, waiting for his next move. His presence casting an unwelcomed shadow as a darkness filled the room. What was he thinking?

Then he spoke, his shoulders visibly raised as he drew in a breath. 'I cannot stay here if you don't want me.' He was serious about us being together.

Attempting to salvage the situation using the rational part of my brain. 'Why? There must be a way we can make this work.' A stupid reply, we both knew that wouldn't work.

Nico, shook his head from side to side and I stayed silent. He couldn't even look at me.

'I will go back to Athens to be nearer my family,' he eventually said.

'I should leave, you were here on the island before me.' I didn't want to leave but it sounded the right thing to say at the time.

He turned back to face me. I saw a sadness now around his eyes, I'd not seen before. Was this the real Nico, a vulnerable side I had never witnessed before?

'It is okay, my father is in poor health. It will be beneficial for me to return and support my mother, it has been a number of months since I last visited them,' Nico informed me. I didn't think it appropriate to ask what was wrong with his father.

'When will you leave?'

'It will take me a couple of days to make arrangements, I have a duty to the church and people I serve.'

'Yes of course.' I had no duty to anyone apart from me.

I picked up my cup and drank, needing a pause.

Nico's tea remained untouched.

'You could join me, not straight away, if you change your mind.' One further attempt to sew doubt in my mind. I stayed silent and looked away.

'I will leave you now,' he said when I didn't answer.

Chapter 28

The clatter of a small creature scurrying around on the roof woke me. I didn't hear Jack come home the night before and surmised he must have had an action packed day with Millie. I didn't check in on him either that morning. I felt a bit numb from the previous day's events with Nico and decided it was time to get back to my writing. I needed a distraction.

Coffee pot on and breakfast ready to eat, determined to make the best of the day. I hadn't changed my mind about what I'd said to Nico, even though he had left me with an option to join him. Join him and then what? I put that comment to the back of my mind. And there was still the outstanding issue of George to think through.

Surprisingly I got straight back into the story, the scene I was writing appeared to flow out of me.

I guess I had been working for an hour or so when the sound of footsteps coming down my creaking stairs disturbed my flow and more than one person.

'Hi Sis.'

'Hi there,' Millie said.

'What's for breakfast?' Jack asked.

'Help yourselves, although you may want to make fresh coffee.' I didn't mind Millie staying they were grown adults after all, but it would have been nice to have been asked. Although it couldn't have been comfortable for them squeezing into a single bed, the size of Jack. That's if they did much sleeping!

Jack busied himself getting food for them both, Millie took his usual seat at the table, which gave me a chance to speak with her. I hadn't been given the opportunity before, Jack reluctant to introduce us.

'So Millie, have you had chance to think about what you are likely to do when you get back to England?' She glanced over towards Jack as if she required his permission to answer.

'Not entirely,' she said.

'Any jobs you fancy doing?'

Millie's right hand moved to a gold chain around her neckline, she held the tiny charm between her thumb and first finger. 'A couple,' she replied and gave a nervous smile.

I backed off, not wanting to scare her. 'Oh, plenty of time I guess.'

It was hard work trying to get a conversation going. I suspected they were keeping something from me by the glances shared between them. Jack eventually sat down and they ate their breakfast. I didn't speak and neither did they. Fortunately, the awkwardness interrupted by the sound of a car outside and a door shutting, followed by a knock at the door. I guessed it was George coming to pick up his daughter.

'I'll get it,' Jack said, bounding to the door.

George stood side-on in the doorway. His usual confident stance less pronounced. He glanced passed Jack and raised a hand to acknowledge my presence. I smiled and raised my hand in response but feeling a bucket full of guilt. Actually, that was an understatement.

Millie stood from the table. 'Thanks for breakfast Kate.' And she left.

Jack returned from the door. 'What have you got planned for today?'

'Never mind that, what about this relationship with Millie?'

'What about it?'

'Is it getting serious?'

'Hardly, I've barely known her a week.'

'She shared a bed with you last night.' How hypocritical of me to say that, if only he knew what his sister had done and with a priest of all people. I hoped my face didn't flush with the guilt I concealed.

'I do like her, a lot as it happens.' Jack forced a grin. 'But its early days.'

'So how long is she staying here with her father?' Hopeful Jack's answer would give me a pretty good idea as to how long he was hanging around.

'Not sure, but I do have some other information which you will be delighted about,' he quickly replied and seated himself in his usual chair.

'And what is that exactly?' I asked, trying to show interest.

'Sarah is leaving on a plane,' he paused, 'tonight. George and Millie are taking her to the airport.'

'Oh I see, so soon.'

'Not, ooh that's good news.' Jack appeared disappointed with my response judging by his childish reply, which I found somewhat irritating.

I was surprised Sarah was leaving so soon, and

wondered what George had told her for her to finally get the message and he could resume the new life he had come here for. Unless he did end up booking a flight for her and she was forced to leave. Now she was leaving, I didn't know how long he would wait for me to contact him and wasn't sure I could face him, even though I knew what Sarah had done.

Jack brought me back from my pondering. 'Fancy a swim?'

'What now?'

'Yes come on, it will be fun.' Jack's face filled with a big grin.

'Okay,' I said reluctantly.

I have to say I was feeling bashful about Jack seeing me in my costume. I know he is my brother, but we hadn't seen each other in what is essentially underwear since our younger days. Jack had nothing to worry about, he'd caught a great tan on his muscled body in the short time he had been staying with me.

We grabbed towels and headed down to the sea. I didn't have much choice of getting in gradually, Jack scooped me up and threw me in.

'Right you are in big trouble now,' I said managing to get to my feet, wiping the salty taste from my mouth.

Jack came further into the water and I set off to chase after him but he was too fast. I lost my footing, the sand sliding beneath me and ended up under the water again. Jack held his sides in hysterics and I joined in seeing the funny side. Just like that we were suddenly kids again.

We stayed in the sea for quite some time, a chance for me to forget my other scenarios. Jack couldn't help himself by showing me he could still do a decent butterfly stroke as he pounded the water. I was quite content with my breast stroke, avoiding the need to take in any more salt water.

I thought of my dad as I pushed against the water, and how he first taught me to swim in the sea before Jack was born. Dad was a terrific swimmer and I am sure Jack inherited his talent for it from him, certainly wasn't from mum because she couldn't swim.

Hopping from one foot to the other across the scorching sand, we made our way to our towels to allow our bodies dry in the late morning sun.

'It's been great having you here Jack.'

'Really?' His voice higher.

'Yes, its been fun.' Although his timing not the best, granted. Yet, if he hadn't been staying I wouldn't have been able to spend a day like this, giving me a much needed distraction.

'Thanks, I'm having a great time.' He shook his head releasing the water from his blond locks, some of which landed on me. Jack reminded me of a dog fresh out of a pond.

'Good,' I replied.

Jack brushed the grains of sand from his large feet as he spoke. 'I am not denying that I did think you were a bit bonkers when you left England to come and live here, especially as you didn't know a sole. I presumed it would be really boring and you would be shut off from civilisation. The only things I could find out about this place was sponges and rock climbing.'

'I have a sponge, although I haven't tried to rock climb yet.'

Jack smiled at my comment.

'I can see why you like this island and the people here,' he said.

'I'm glad I have your seal of approval.'

Jack picked up a small stone, he turned it over in his fingers, and threw it into the sea. 'Paul would approve of you living here too.'

I felt a lump in my throat and my eyes glazed over, unable to look Jack's way. We hadn't spoken of Paul since Jack arrived. I hadn't intentionally hidden my emotions away, I couldn't speak for Jack of course. Had he been waiting for the right moment to mention Paul's name?

A silence fell between us. Jack picked up another stone and it disappeared out of sight. Perhaps Jack was remembering the fun times they shared.

Composing myself. 'So what's next for you?'

Jack rolled onto his side towards me. 'I was thinking of asking George if I could work at his vineyard for a bit until I decide what I want to do.' So he was staying longer.

'What about Millie?'

'She's staying too obviously.'

'You've no plans to return to England for a while then?'

'Not if George is happy with our suggestion. I think he will be thrilled Millie wants to stay now Sarah is out of the way. Gives them time to hang out.'

My arms felt hot and starting to look red as I held them out in front of me. 'Found out much about Millie?'

'Yes,' he answered back.

'Anything interesting?'

Jack rolled onto his back and lent back on his arms, stretching his tanned legs out on the sand. He kept the suspense going, his eyes set straight ahead.

'She's had one serious relationship. A guy called

Mark and they met at Uni.'

'Oh, just the one?' Millie was very pretty and I was surprised by Jack's response.

Jack raised his eyebrows. 'He was one of her lecturers.'

I couldn't stop my mouth from gaping wide.

'You can shut your mouth now,' Jack said, turning his head my way and continued, 'yep, ten years older apparently.' Perhaps not that shocking, it was roughly the same age difference between Millie and Jack, although Jack didn't look his age.

'Well that's not ethical behaviour,' I replied, unless the rules were different at university. It didn't happen in my day, although if I recall they appeared much older and not good looking. How did they kept their relationship a secret I wondered?

Jack remained silent.

'How long was this relationship?' I asked leaning back on my towel.

'Three years Millie said.'

'Did anyone know about it?'

'Nope.'

'Sounds odd don't you think?'

Jack shrugged his shoulders. 'He had a campervan and they went away a lot in that, far away from

Bath.' That made sense away from prying eyes.

I started to get an image in my head of this Mark, older guy seducing a younger girl, his dirty secret. Did he pursue her and even stalk her? Well this was an interesting tale and I was drawn in.

'What did she tell her friends, they must have wondered why she wasn't seeing anyone?'

'I asked the same question. She told them she had a boyfriend back home.' A plausible explanation.

'How did it end with this Mark?'

Jack let out a sigh. 'It hasn't officially, yet.'

'Really, does he know she is here?'

'Yes, but I'm not sure she told him the name of the island,' Jack stated.

I raised a hand to my forehead and massaged the skin between my fingers hoping we didn't get another unexpected visitor. 'Well I wasn't expecting you to tell me this. I assume George has no idea?'

'No, Sarah neither. In fact Sarah hinted Millie might be gay since she hadn't met any boyfriends. Of course Millie put Sarah straight knowing how disapproving she would be if she found out her daughter had a girlfriend. So Millie sent Sarah a photo of her and Mark together, she made up a story that he worked in a bar near where she lived.'

'Is she still in love with him?'

'No,' Jack answered with certainty.

'How do you know?'

'She told me. And she has me now.' Of course silly me, who could resist Jack. I recalled the earlier conversation we had about snorkelling and the water bike and realised Jack had a motive to impress Millie. Maybe this the first time he had encountered competition, in the back of his mind doubting if Millie was going to finish her relationship once and for all.

I decided we'd talked enough about this subject, not wanting to push Jack further and reverted back to our previous conversation of him working for George at the vineyard.

'Anyway, I'm sure George will enjoy having Millie around, however I am not sure about you,' I said springing to my feet, grabbing my towel and attempted to race back to the house before Jack could catch me. I had no chance against those long legs, he grabbed hold of me and before I knew it I was upside down over his shoulder, the rush of blood quickly filling my head. This display for all to see he was finally in charge and not me.

We didn't do much for the rest of the day, although I did manage a smidge more writing. Jack picked up my book about Kalymnos and read that for most of the afternoon. He appeared to be serious about staying, reading up on the history of the island.

It became just the sort of day I needed, relaxed and uncomplicated, especially after recent events. Certain I wouldn't see George again that day as he delivered Sarah to the airport, I wasn't sure if I would see Nico ever again and my feelings were not settled about him.

Chapter 29

I'd said earlier that the following two weeks after Jack arrived were going to be eventful and thus far they had. I woke up deciding a need for calmer seas was required to balance the disorder in my life. There was however, something I needed to find out to ensure closure in my mind. When would Nico be leaving the island? How could I find out? I contemplated going to the church and perhaps hiding behind some bushes or the large tree, to see if he entered or left. I thought about going into the town, getting close enough to his house and taking cover. Perhaps I had watched too many private detective films, my imagination running away with me. Then the answer came to me and it was obvious: Aella, she knew about everything and everyone it appeared. Although, she didn't know the name of the man I had slept with and never likely to. I called and she answered.

'Hi Aella, how are you?'

'I am great, how about you?'

What I wanted to say was my mind was still unsettled. 'I'm feeling more myself Aella.'

'Good.' Her tone flat. I hadn't spoken to Aella since my lift home and realised I should have sent her a text message or called. She continued, 'I hear Sarah left last night on a plane back to England.' Aella's sources had not let her down.

'So I understand from Jack.' I needed to move her off the subject of Sarah and George and on to finding out about Nico.

'Aella, just wondered if you heard what had happened to the priest Nicolaos?' I used his full name as I wasn't certain if it was only me who called him Nico. Oh and Jack, though I don't think he was given permission.

'Why? I thought you knew him better than I.'

'No reason, I overheard somebody outside the church saying he was leaving or had left the island.'

'Oh yes, now I remember.' Remembered what?

'I heard he was returning back home, Athens. Something about a sick father,' Aella said. So it was true what he told me. I had no reason to believe he would lie to me, but it was reassuring to hear confirmation, I suspected Aella's sources were rarely wrong.

'Oh.' I said casually. 'I wonder how long he will be gone.'

'I got the impression he would not be coming back for some time or ever. There is another priest coming to take his place.'

The line went quiet and I wasn't sure whether to push my luck and ask another question. I didn't need to think of another one, Aella was a step ahead of me.

'Why do you not know this, he was at your house the other day.'

I rambled back a response. 'He didn't mention anything. We were not that friendly, only occasionally he would call and say hello on his way back from visiting a sick man near to where I live.' I held my phone away from my face, filled my lungs and exhaled. There was truth in that, the sick man he visited when Jack saw him.

'Such a handsome man,' she said aloud, a small sigh just audible.

And then an uncomfortable silence until I spoke. 'Jack is talking about staying longer.'

'Oh great news I like Jack.'

'Yes I know you do.' The feeling mutual for Jack but I didn't tell her that.

'It is good for you to have him around.'

'Yes, I am enjoying his company. That's when he's not out with Millie.'

'They look cute together, let him have his fun.' She was right and after all I wasn't his mother, although the way I had been questioning Jack lately it probably felt for him I could be.

'When are you seeing George?' Aella asked. I was astounded she presumed I would move on so quickly, especially after the news I shared with her.

'Aella, he has only just got rid of his wife.'

'She is not really his wife. You must not let him wait too long, he will find someone else.'

'I will speak to him soon, I promise.' I was pretty certain George wasn't in a rush based on recent events and that could definitely be said for me. I wanted to find out what truly happened between George and Sarah and tell him about the visit she paid me but then questioned if it mattered. I knew the truth now or perhaps part of it.

'Okay make sure you do, I have to go now Stephon is calling me,' Aella replied and we said our goodbyes.

I wondered if she were using Stephon as an excuse, still disappointed I hadn't confided in her. When I thought back, I'm surprised I told her. Then again, I wasn't myself that day. At least now I knew for certain Nico was definitely leaving. It still wasn't clear though if he had actually gone, but I suspected he wouldn't want to hang around. I was alerted at that moment I may never see him again. The walks back from the market, followed by the talks we shared drinking tea sat at my table. The flowers which were still flourishing, planted by his hands. It saddened me to think I had lost a true friend. I couldn't believe we had taken it to the next level. The forbidden level.

I became restless and as Jack was out again with Millie I had nothing to occupy my mind and appeared in no state to write. I couldn't stay at home while I was feeling this way, so I ventured out to let the sunshine improve my mood.

Before long I found myself standing outside the church. Nico's church. I walked through the gate and sat on the well-used wooden bench. The one Nico and I chatted on, while I contemplated what to do next. I hadn't intentionally gone there but that was where my unsettled mind had taken me. I plainly had no desire to go inside the holy place with the guilt I carried around like a sack of potatoes on my back. My eyes were drawn towards the large tree, remembering the boys playing beneath it.

A coughing noise disrupted my thoughts. An elderly lady shuffled out of the church and despite the fact she was notably hunched over, her hair was dark without a hint of grey. Which is more than I could say for myself, as I suspected all of the stress I'd put my body through recently, was going to start showing some signs of premature ageing.

She didn't see me sitting against the sun-baked church wall and I wondered if Nico were inside. 'I would give it all up for you,' he had said. His words dramatic.

I sat for another five minutes in a daze until disturbed. A lone hen approached from somewhere, pecking close to my feet. Its visit prompted me to be on my way not really knowing where I was heading.

My feet led me back to the sanctuary of my house and as I approached something lay half tucked under the well-trodden mat at my door. A folded piece of paper, it had to be from Nico and he had left it and gone. I glanced at the bottom.

Kate,

Sorry I missed you! I guess Jack has told you Sarah has gone back to England. Millie has told me she would like to stick around for a while on the island, Jack too. They want me to give them work at the vineyard. I am happy for this to happen, there are plenty of jobs to be done. I assume you are ok with this?

I hope to see you soon.

George x

Ps when you are ready

The note although brief, cheered me up. I decided it was for the best to put Nico out of my mind. He was leaving and we didn't need to see each other again.

I looked at the note again and had an idea, I would plan the task that George had given me of sorting out our next adventure. I picked up my book about the island and buried myself in it to see where I could take him.

I found a few options to choose from and I jotted them down. Pothia was at the top of my list, and although I was tempted to return, I crossed that off my list. A boat trip to the island of Telendos looked promising, until I read on and learnt it favoured naturist beaches. I crossed that one out and chose Kefalas cave. Apparently the most impressive and beautiful cave on the entire island of Kalymnos and the best way to get there by boat as the road apparently became a dirt road.

This was just the distraction I needed. My mood lifted and feeling spontaneous I decided to call George. A flaw in this plan as I didn't have his number, we had always met in person when I thought about it. Not put off by this significant technicality I called Aella on her mobile, no answer and then her home number and no success there either. I wasn't confident Aella would have his number anyway and I didn't want her to bother Stavros for it. I tried Jack next and he picked up straight away.

'Hey, you okay sis?' I detected concern in Jack's voice.

'Yes, I'm fine. Are you with Millie?' Stupid question, I knew he was.

'Yes.'

Clearing my throat with a forced cough. 'I don't suppose you could ask her for George's number.'

'You haven't got it.' Jack's voice sounded surprised.

'Obviously I haven't got it that's why I am calling you.'

The line went quiet.

'Why do you need it?' Jack was making me work for this request.

'I just do Jack, stop messing about.'

'Okay, keep your hair on. I'll get it off Millie and text it to you.'

'Thank you. Oh and Jack, enjoy your day with Millie.'

'Sure.'

I waited for the number to ping through staring at the screen, expecting it to happen immediately. How long did it take for heaven's sake? I suspected Jack had to explain why he wanted it and Millie was asking why I wanted it. My phone flashed and I sighed with relief.

After I saved the number into my phone I called and awaited his answer. I didn't want things to move too fast with George at this stage, especially after all of the highs and lows' recently but I knew I wanted to spend more time with him. Six rings and his answer message kicked in.

'This is George Harris, leave a message and the best number to make contact with you.'

My mind went blank for at least 5 seconds and then finding courage to speak. 'George its Kate, I have arranged our day out I mean adventure for tomorrow if you are free. I'll understand if you are busy it is short notice.' I was cut off by a beeping sound. I made myself call the number again and waited for his message to finish.

'Hi, it's me again, Kate. Can you meet me at the bus station at 8:50am. Oh, and wear comfortable shoes.' There it was done.

Why did I say 'comfortable shoes'? He wasn't an old man. I shook my head and smiled. I turned on the radio and made a sandwich, tapping my feet to the upbeat tune. I opened a beer and chilled on my worn out sofa looking forward to my day with George. So his surname was Harris, it hadn't occurred to me I didn't know his full name.

I sent a text to Aella. "Fingers crossed, out with George tomorrow!"

Her response within seconds. "Good"

Chapter 30

I woke up early, and sprang out of bed. As I drew back the curtains, dark clouds occupied the sky. A rare sight. I hoped it wasn't a bad omen for my trip planned with George.

I showered, dressed in shorts and a t-shirt, and changed my mind to a linen shirt in case it became chilly in the caves. I lightly knocked on Jack's door and as I expected no response. When I opened the door his bed lay empty. He stayed with Millie of course.

I grabbed a banana and a bottle of water from my now depleted fridge. Because I had been trying to avoid Nico I hadn't shopped for a few days. I headed into the town and kept focussed on the way ahead without glancing at his church.

I found the bus station fairly empty when I arrived, glancing at my watch it was only 8:45am, perhaps too early for some. I took a seat waiting for George and noticed the clouds had lifted, our island bathed in uninterrupted sunshine once again. I realised I should have said in the phone message to call or text me back to confirm, that would have been the logical thing to do. That I presumed he could just drop everything to meet me at short notice perhaps a naive assumption.

8:55am and still no sign of George. Damn it I thought, I shouldn't have assumed he would come, probably busy working or maybe he had changed his mind about me.

The bus driver had let all of the passengers on until I was left waiting. He kept staring at me through his dark eyes and big bushy brows, as if to say 'are you getting on or not?' I stood and stepped on, I had nothing else planned for the day. I paid my fare to the driver and gave him a forced smile.

I promptly took a seat sensing the driver was now ready to make his move, then I contemplated getting off the bus, changing my mind about doing the trip on my own. I just got to my feet as the driver pulled away so I sat back in my seat.

The bus came to an abrupt stop jolting me forward. The other passengers now looking to see what he may have hit. The doors opened and George stepped on. I breathed out in relief as he came to join me.

'You made it.'

There was a nasty red scratch below his left cheek bone ending near the corner of his mouth. I didn't know what to say, George gave me a slow and deliberate wink.

'So tell me, what you have planned, where are we going?' George asked curiously.

'Wait and see,' I replied and turned my face to look out of the window.

George was keen to chat, however I found it hard to ignore the scratch on his face. He tried to guess where we were heading, without success, and it was difficult to focus on his questions when what I really wanted to ask him was how he got the scratch. Whether he got into a row with Sarah and she had left her mark on him. George stopped speaking and we both sat quietly for the rest of the short bus journey until the next part of our journey by sea.

After a short walk from the bus stop we found the waterfront kiosk where boat trips could be hired. I gave my name to the skipper of our boat. George stepped on first and held out his hand to help me board the small vessel and we took our seats. I smiled to myself noticing George had swapped his shiny shoes for a more casual pair and as always he smelt amazing.

'I'm thinking of acquiring a boat,' George whispered into my ear. I regarded George with a quizzical look, was he being serious? Although, a real possibility he would want to add to his transport collection no doubt.

The boat ride took us another fifteen minutes around the rugged coastline until we arrived at our destination near to Pothia. There happened to be six other people who had chosen to take the same trip and after a short walk, we along with the other visitors climbed a few steps to the entrance.

'Here we are at Kefalas cave.' Actually I didn't have to announce it, we found a large sign clearly telling us. When I am nervous, I have a tendency to state the obvious most people keep within the confines of their mind, Paul often teased me about it.

'I've heard about this place from Stavros,' George was quick to point out.

'It contains six inner chambers and huge stalagmites and stalactites. Apparently we will be able to see traces of the worship of Zeus. Did you know that it is also known as the Cave of Zeus?'

'No I did not. You have been busy researching this place, I'm impressed,' George said with a nod of his head.

George stepped towards a man standing close

by and handed over his phone.

'This is worth a photo surely,' he said returning to my side. 'Let's stand by the sign.'

George placed his arm around my shoulder. 'Say cheese.'

I smiled for the photo. Our first together.

On first entering the cave we met with darkness, our bodies shuffling forward, my shoulder brushing against George gently as my body met with a reluctance to go into the unknown. The bright yellow hard helmets we had to wear subtly lighting the way with their small spot lights. The scene reminding me of old pictures I had seen of miners, having to endure the confines of a pit.

'Okay?' George whispered into my ear.

'Yes,' I replied back reassuring him.

Quickly, certain parts were cleverly lit to add to the atmosphere and I was glad of this as it became a bit claustrophobic in places. For me anyway. The rock had many different colours: white, grey, golds and browns. Icicle shaped rock, some thick others thin with pointed tips, hung from the ceiling of the cave and in other places rocks rose up from the cave floor. I didn't know the difference between stalagmites and stalactites but concluded it must be something to do with the way they formed, upwards versus downwards. As I pondered this I lost my footing. George's reactions were lightening quick, grabbing for my hand and at the same time his other arm slipped around my waist bringing us face to face.

I was vaguely aware of other voices bouncing off the cave walls, but my body now paying full attention to the nearness to George. He released his arm but his warm hand held on to mine. I didn't let go, it felt good. We caught up with our group.

Our tour over, we stepped out into bright sunshine and looking down I released my hold from George's hand. A small shed like structure selling refreshments stood close by and we strolled towards it grabbing a light snack and a cold drink.

'Kate, what do you think about Jack and Millie's relationship?' George asked as we walked a few steps to a wall and I perched myself upon the hard grey stone.

'Is it a relationship or a holiday romance?' I didn't mean to sound flippant but that is how it probably came across. Surprised George wanted to talk about Jack and Millie, I presumed the day was about us.

George eventually sat next to me, a few inches separating us. 'Jack's okay, I think Millie is quite keen on him.' I was surprised George would be so relaxed about his daughter's relationships. Jack did have a number of years on Millie and quite a few conquests under his belt. I decided it was for the best not to inform George of those. To be honest I wouldn't know where to start and that was just the ones I knew about. I also kept quiet about the lecturer called Mark. What a fitting description.

'So, they are going to work for you for a while.'

'Looks that way. Jack can stay at my place if he is getting under your feet,' George said and smiled. I accepted my house was on the small size however, I had got use to Jack being around.

Lightening my tone so I didn't sound like a killjoy. 'It's up to him, I'm easy either way after all he is an adult.' I flashed a smile back his way.

I had a sneaking feeling Jack would most likely float between the two houses if I was honest, for that matter Millie too if she was prepared to put up with a single bed. In fact I did need to give the sleeping arrangements some consideration if Jack was staying longer. Jack hadn't complained once about the bed being too small, and seeing that he was being such a good house guest, I supposed I could consider giving him my room. It wasn't a bad thing having Jack and Millie around, it would ensure I didn't take things too quickly with George. Assuming he wanted to see me again. I was secretly praying he would.

By the time we'd taken the boat back and a bus

to our town, the sun's bright yellow glow now less intense as it retired for the night. A welcoming gentle breeze greeted us as we walked into the square. George suggested we grab a drink at Kali Orexi before we ended the day. He told me he had left his car parked nearby.

We ordered red wine and were tempted by cooking smells filling the air so we decided to order food too, which I was glad of, remembering I needed to replenish my fridge.

'What do you fancy?' George asked, perusing his menu.

'Meze would be good.'

'Great choice.'

The waiter suggested we try the Dolmades and expertly described how the vine leaves were exceptionally tender and perfectly encased the rice and fresh herbs. George asked for Spanakopita Triangles as they were his favourite and coincidently one of mine too.

The day was going extremely well, after it started out with uncertainty. I mentally congratulated myself for my well executed planning skills and sensed George was having a good time too.

George leant forward, tapping his finger on his lips, teasing me to ask what was on his mind. I sat back into my chair and tried to stare him out.

He succumbed first and laughed. 'When am I going to see you in that headscarf again?'

A smirk developed on my face and I casually took a sip of my wine, then I responded. 'Wishing you had bought one now?'

George raised his fair eyebrows. 'They didn't stock my colour.'

The waiter reappeared balancing our food and I was famished to the point my stomach was rumbling. Hopefully not loud enough for George to hear. I took a bite into one of the triangles, its tangy spinach and feta mixture tasted absolutely delicious. I dabbed my napkin around my mouth, not wanting a repeat of the last time I ate with George.

We were in no rush to go anywhere else, I definitely wasn't as George appeared in a flirty mood, his chat light and fun. He reminded me of Paul in that way. Then the unthinkable happened.

He walked from the direction of his house. Stupid really, that I hadn't accepted he might still be on the island. He looked from side to side taking in his surroundings, carrying a hefty suitcase. This was it, he was actually leaving. Unable to watch him go, but found I couldn't avert my eyes. It didn't seem real and my body tensed, my hands clasped tightly in my lap as he came closer.

About to make my excuses to George that I needed to visit the loo, when Nico looked our way and came to a halt. Our stares locked for a couple of seconds and then he glanced at George and carried on his way. Nico turned the corner, out of my sight.

I closed my eyes, breathed through my nose and let the air out slowly through pursed lips. I opened my eyes and reached for my glass and drank a large gulp of wine.

'Are you okay?' George asked.

Placing my glass down, I gave George my full attention and smiled at him, convincingly acting as though nothing had happened.

Nico had left the island.

We stepped out of the taverna after I insisted on paying for our meal. George was not happy about it, until I pointed out he paid last time.

'My car is over there.' George pointed to a street a few feet away and I could just see a glimpse of its red body, the last of the sunlight bouncing off the shiny metal bumper.

'I'm going to walk George, it's a lovely night.'

After such a great day, an awkward moment occurred as we stayed rooted to the spot. George stepped closer and took both my hands in his. His thumbs caressed the backs of my hands and I looked into the brightness of his eyes.

'Thanks for a great day, it was worth the wait.' George leant forward and I closed my eyes. His lips smooth and warm on my cheek. As he withdrew, my lids gently opened to find his handsome face smiling at me.

'Of course it was worth the wait.' I returned the kiss back on his cheek, the one without the mark. George still hadn't mentioned anything about how it happened and perhaps better left that way.

Reluctantly I released my hands and started on my walk home. I turned back and he stood in the same place. I waved and he waved back and I continued on my way. Satisfied I had cleverly hid my emotions from George, seeing Nico for the last time. I didn't want anything to spoil my day with George, he didn't deserve that.

Nico had gone, presumably forever. What must he have assumed when he saw me sitting with George? Did he recognise George? Why would he, to my knowledge they had never met. Although he had seen us drinking coffee in the square, the dreaded day when I first met Sarah and Millie. Perhaps Nico questioned why I had moved on from him so quickly. But I wasn't in a relationship with Nico, what happened shouldn't have happened. Nico once told me he moved to Kalymnos to avoid 'further distractions', I wished I'd found out what that meant. Was I just another one to add to his many? Was I an unfulfilled passion? What did it matter now anyway, asking these pointless questions. I had no way of finding out now and without doubt his departure made things final between us. I needed to take things slowly with George and not rush into anything. Although my feelings for George were intensifying.

When I arrived back, the house was in darkness. I turned on a light and found Jack lounging on the sofa. He looked like he had just awoken from a snooze, stretching his long arms above his head.

'Good day, sis?'

How did I answer? Simply. 'Yes, and you?'

'Excellent. Where have you been, you look quite tired?'

'Out with George.'

'Oh yes of course, tell me all about it then.' Jack patted the seat beside him.

'I'm bushed, how about we have a catch up over breakfast in the morning and I'll tell you all then.' I truly was bushed from all the intensity and adrenalin flowing through my body.

'Okay see you in the morning. Oh Kate.'

'Yes.'

'Is there a secret stash of beer?'

'No Jack, you will have to do with tea instead.'

I trudged up the stairs to my bed, physically

and emotionally drained from the day's events. I didn't have the energy to step out of my clothes and fell asleep on top of the bed.

Chapter 31

Since Jack landed on my doorstep unannounced, it was astounding to me when I reflected on what had taken place in such a short period of time. I certainly hadn't anticipated this level of activity when I left England to come and live here.

The last two weeks had been a mix of emotions, at times felt like I was enduring a rollercoaster ride, with me in the front carriage. Some parts were funny, for instance seeing Nico unexpectedly in his shorts and remembering Jack in hysterics down at the water, although at my expense. Other parts filled with romance and passion from both George and Nico. My adventures out with George which made me appreciate the island and him even more. Then sadness and relief when Nico left the island, I deduced forever. Unplanned arrivals from Jack and Millie. Not forgetting Sarah. If George had taken her back and she'd stayed,

I couldn't say with certainty I would have contained the green-eyed monster within me. Spending lots of welcomed time with Jack, I am so glad he came even though his timing wasn't the best. My friends Aella and Stavros providing the hospitality, however not knowing the full story of what had occurred between me and Nico, just as well. I hoped Stavros was still in the dark about my sexual liaison, I presumed Aella kept some secrets from him. Deep down I wondered if Aella suspected it could be Nico and she was tempted to raise the subject again. Perhaps she had wanted to ask me who my secret lover was but respected my privacy as the true friend she is.

'Where is that breakfast you promised me?' Jack barked out his order and stopped my reflective mood in its tracks.

I cracked the eggs into a bowl and whisked, adding ham to make omelettes. As the smell from the frying pan filled the air, I began to tell Jack about our visit to Kefalas cave as promised. He seemed genuinely interested, asking questions and I answered them with the new knowledge I had gained. Jack impressed by this said he would definitely take Millie there.

We took our plated food out to the garden and in between mouthfuls chatted about him staying and working for George at his vineyard.

'I bet you didn't see that career change in your life plan,' I stated.

'How's that then?'

'Office work swapped for manual labour and big city living downsized to a small town.'

'Nope.'

'George told me you could live in too.'

Jack halted his fork before it entered his mouth. 'I'd rather stay with you, just in case.' I assumed he meant in case it didn't work out with Millie rather than working for George and I suspected he would stay over at George's place whenever the opportunity arose.

Jack told me he was surprised to find George laid back about their relationship and he didn't want to overstep the mark. After all George was giving him a job. It appeared Jack could be honourable and grown up when he wanted to be, better late than never.

Jack hadn't asked me about Nico's sudden departure and I surmised he hadn't heard of that particular piece of news yet. I was sure it wouldn't take long for him to find out, news appeared to travel fast in our town. At least there was a legitimate reason I could give him if he questioned me about it. Jack didn't appear to take to Nico and I wondered if he had a sixth sense about him.

My brother patted his stomach and gave a satisfied grin. 'Do you know what would have made this even better?'

'Do tell.'

'Tomato ketchup.' I hadn't thought about it, but because Jack had pointed it out my taste buds were sending a signal to my brain.

Jack raised his hands to the top of his head. 'I completely forgot.' He sprung from his chair and went inside the house. I was still thinking of ketchup, smothered over bacon on thick white crusty bread.

A few moments later he returned and placed the yellow box on the table.

'A gift, better late than never.' Twining's English breakfast tea. I didn't have the heart to tell him I had weaned myself from it.

As I washed and Jack dried, something we had naturally fallen into when he was around, I told him I was fine about his plans, concealing how pleased I was he was staying longer. I had moved to the island to find a different life and it appeared Jack was finding one too. I reflected for a moment how sad that family members can drift apart, not intentionally but like a tree forming branches, growing in different directions, responding to seasons and adjusting as time goes by.

Then back to the task as I placed the final plate in Jack's hand and promptly informed him he needed to chip in and buy provisions too, now he was staying longer. I wasn't made of money!

The following two weeks settled down a little until our next gathering.

'Ready?' I asked Jack.

'Absolutely.'

As we approached the main beach by the town, the night's sky now turning to dusk as the yellow sun faded away. The brightness of naked flames flickered, not just in one place but randomly dotted around the beach. A smell of burnt wood filling the air.

'Kate, Jack, over here,' Aella called, alongside Stavros and Stephon by one of the many small crackling bonfires.

Earlier that day Aella had called. 'Are you going to the beach tonight?'

'The beach.' What was she talking about?

'Yes, the beach. It is the Feast of Agios Ioannus.' Aella expected me to know who and what she was referring to. She didn't take my silence as being none the wiser.

'Aella I don't know who this person is.'

A frustrated outbreath of air. 'Certainly you do. John the Baptist, we are celebrating his birth date.'

'Oh yes, I know him well enough.' Aella blind to my amused smile.

'We will meet you both at the beach, 8pm. And afterwards we feast and celebrate in the square.'

'Okay,' I replied intrigued by the event.

Stephon jumped up and down, a ball of energy; excited by the sights and sounds around him, keen to escape from his father's large hand as he attempted to pull free. Excitable teenagers jumped over small fires, shouting out to each other. I wondered how long this tradition had been held. How many generations stood here before? Perhaps Stavros had been here alongside his father soaking up the atmosphere or even jumped with his friends over the flames.

'This happens in all parts of Greece,' Stavros told me. 'You do this for Guy Fawkes.'

'Yes not quite the same though Stavros and usually not on a beach,' I replied.

'This is a flurry of activity.' I didn't need to turn around to recognise his voice. Millie quickly moved to stand by Jack, her face lighting up at the sight of him. Jack placed one of his long arms around her shoulder and squeezed her petite frame into his side.

'Tempted to have a go?' George directed his question at Jack. For a moment Jack looked as if he might take the bait and then he shook his head from side to side.

'How about you Stavros?' George now looking across to Stavros.

'Ha, in my younger days,' Stavros replied.

George stepped closer to me. I smiled at him waiting for him to speak. He looked down to his hand and turned his palm, I placed my hand in his. This the first time, showing our affection for each other in front of our family and friends. We'd been texting each other since our visit to the caves, but hadn't managed to hook up again in person. George had been busy with work travelling and promised to make it up to me. I was quite happy texting and looked forward to his daily message. George had told Millie we were growing close, although I suspect Jack probably beat him to it, I had carelessly left my phone on the kitchen table.

Aella glanced our way, her eyes falling to our hands as she gave one of her smug smiles.

'Fancy a stroll?' George whispered into my ear.

'Yes,' I kicked off my sandals.

The night's air hit my senses, a mixture of smoke reminding me of bonfire night and also hints of saltiness as we walked closer to the water's edge. The magnificent moon gave the dark sea a sprinkling of light; a magical sight. George let go of my hand and placed his arm around my shoulder as if it were meant to be. I let my head fall against his chest, his heart beating slow and strong. We didn't speak, it wasn't necessary and my body relaxed into his, both oblivious to the excitement behind us.

'Hey you two it is time to go to the square,' Stavros shouted. George slipped his hand in mine and we returned to our group.

Stavros tickled Stephon until he squealed and lifted his son onto his broad shoulders, Aella walked by their side. Jack and Millie followed and lastly me and George at the rear. His hand reluctant to let go of mine as we made our way across the sand.

The smell of roasting pork filled the air as we approached the square and not one but three pigs roasted slowly, turning on their giant metal rods over hot flames. A large stage had been erected where upon the band played and a man and woman sang. The celebration already underway, families and friends had taken their seats at long tables and others had started dancing, their arms entwined.

'Hey, is that the old guy we met at Aella's dinner party?' Jack asked. I looked up to find a man in a flat cap dancing on his own, a small crowd stood by encouraging him, clapping to the rhythm of the music. His stance vaguely similar.

We danced, we laughed and ate well while we celebrated the famous Saint. I wondered if life could get any better.

Chapter 32

Birds are chirping and there is a gentle lapping of small waves hitting the sand. Obviously I am standing in my favourite spot, trusted sunhat on and feet cooling in the sea. The temperature has been hitting the mid-eighties of late, so this is a good time to enjoy the early morning sun.

What can I tell you? Well, Jack is still my part-time lodger and I can't believe two months has flown by. Even though he has been working at the vineyard and not forgetting his new girlfriend, we have managed to spend time together. I've even managed to cajole him into helping with some well overdue painting in the house, his height especially useful for those areas well out of my reach. I guess I should think about attempting my garden at some point, plenty of time for that.

Jack is talking passionately about going backpacking with Millie, they haven't agreed on the geographical areas yet, still I suspect Jack will talk her around to his way of thinking. He appears keen to visit Australia and handy that we have distant relatives who live there. I am glad for Jack and why not when he seemingly has no ties. Although I haven't checked his phone recently! I actually feel a pang of jealousy when he tells me where he would like to visit and the wildlife he is hoping to see. But not the huge spiders he is likely to face, they are enough to put me off visiting. I will definitely miss him being around my place when he decides to leave and suspect he will want to come back to visit me and the new friends he has made. Jack is a popular guy and will be missed by all.

I have got to know Millie too after a slow start and have had some interesting conversations with her of late. She isn't the wallflower I assumed her to be. There is no question George has enjoyed having her around. I wonder if Jack has told Millie I know of her secret relationship with Mark. In fact Jack hasn't mentioned it again, and I can only assume when Millie ended the relationship once and for all it went okay. If it hadn't, I guess we may have had another visitor.

And George, he is both relieved and delighted Sarah signed the divorce papers when she returned to England. I am left wondering how he managed to get her to finally sign. He truly is a free agent now, that's the important thing and I suspect Sarah won't be on her own for too long, she is an attractive woman after all. Perhaps in time George might want to talk about what happened between them, but now is not the time to open up old wounds, especially as he has received more great news. George has been approached to appear in a life style magazine after a professional wine taster gave him a glowing review. George told me the editor wants to interview him in Kalymnos and take photographs for the feature. I offered my services to grape stomp if it will enhance the image of his business. He told me he would give this considerable thought and then we both had a fit of the giggles.

As for our relationship, I have been seeing George on a regular basis. We have been taking things slowly and have shared a few steamy kisses recently. I get a flurry of butterflies when we meet and feel like a teenager again, however the cooking pot is almost at boiling point I can tell you.

Aella is undoubtedly excited our relationship is blossoming, and she takes great pride in reminding me we wouldn't have met if it hadn't been for her and Stavros. 'He will make a great lover,' she told me. I was too embarrassed to reply. I get the impression from the hints she drops that she believes a wedding will be on the cards. I try to ignore her as best I can and change the subject frequently as it is far too soon to be talking of this. I'm not sure I want to marry again, and I suspect George isn't too fussed either. I am very happy with the way things are developing with George and will not be rushed by Aella.

Anyway, Aella has her own life to focus on now she is expecting again. Yes you read that correctly. A shock to me when she told me the news, assuring me the baby was planned. She is convinced the baby will be a girl on account she is a different shape this time. She has asked my opinion on suitable names, most of which I struggle to pronounce. 'Maybe you should consider it, you are not getting any younger,' she said patting her tummy a couple of times. Whether she meant that statement or not, a baby is definitely not in my future plans. Although on the positive side, at least she pictured I had it in me, to be a mother.

It hasn't been all plain sailing for me, I had quite a scare myself. When I had my unplanned moment of passion with Nico, we didn't think about possible consequences. Being careful certainly didn't come into my mind and I am certain it didn't his. As you can imagine that sent me into a flurry for a couple of days. To find out I was not pregnant, beyond relief.

I received a letter this morning and didn't recognise the hand writing. When I opened the small envelope and teased out the card inside, I found a picture on the front of a garden with a table and two chairs. The scene surrounded by pretty white flowers.

Dear Kate,

I hope you don't mind me writing to you, after what seems quite some time ago to me since I left the island. I realised I should have come and said goodbye to you in person, but I knew deep down I was not strong enough to cope with my feelings for you.

I am still in Athens staying with my mother. Sadly my father passed away peacefully a couple of days ago. Together with the help of my brothers, we are busy preparing for his funeral and the visitors expected at our family home. Even at this time of grief I am glad to be back home. I didn't realise how much I missed the liveliness of the place. It appears its history is still a big draw to tourists from all over the world. I have not returned to my duties yet, though it is my strongest intention.

I wonder if Jack is still staying with you. And if you have finished your book? I think of the island often and the special memories will never be far away from my thoughts.

I hope you are well and content.

Nico

I hadn't foreseen this. I turned the card over, no address. I thought back to when I saw him for the last time, suitcase in hand and whether the sight of me and George together in the taverna had stirred up emotion. I wondered why he felt the need to write and if there was a hidden message in his words as I read it again, or was he simply telling me he was okay and I am still in his thoughts a little. I glanced at the front of the card one last time and gently tore it in half and half again, placing it in the bin.

So peaceful here, I am lucky to live in this fantastic spot. Where was I with my update? Ah yes, George has asked me over to his house tonight and is going to cook me a meal, just the two of us. I suspect George has legendary culinary skills, he appears to do everything else convincingly. We are celebrating the completion of my book, which in all honesty has taken slightly longer due to the hiatus of activity during June. Janet has expressed we need to meet up in England to start planning my next one. I suspect if I don't return there she may invite herself here. I don't think Kalymnos is quite ready for Janet just yet. Although I wonder what Aella would make of her and likewise.

While I am dining in the company of George, Jack has invited Millie over to my house for the night. He has planned a meal and been into town to buy ingredients by himself, which astounded me as he hasn't offered to cook me a meal since he has been here. Admittedly he bought some fish once for us to eat, but that was the only time. Still I'm not the one he is trying to impress. I'm not convinced he can cook, he hasn't asked for any advice from me. Oh and I forgot to mention, he has bought a ton of candles too.

I feel the softness of wet sand as I wiggle my toes in the shallow sea water, and I can tell you I am ready to take my relationship with George a step further. Nico was a friend, nothing more, and I quickly realised George is the one I want to have a long term relationship with. If I am truly honest, he always was. Whenever I am around George I feel alive and I'm excited for what life has in store for us. My intention is to stay over at George's place tonight, I am hoping this is what he wants to, unless I have read all the signs incorrectly. I've even bought new underwear and will be packing a tooth brush in my handbag! That well overdue pedicure and manicure has happened at long last, after all George is an attractive man and I don't want him to look in anyone else's direction. Although, I haven't decided on what I will wear or whether to have my hair up or leave it down. All joking aside, this time it is planned and is why I know I will feel no guilt at all.

Before I head back to the house I take in deep breaths and a few more, my thumb turning my wedding ring back and forth. I wait for a sign, perhaps a bird calling in the distance. Nothing. The only sound, the gentle lapping of the waves.

I close my eyes and his face appears. He is saying my name and I can hear him laughing. We are on holiday on Kalymnos, my visions of him clear and my heart swells. I smile even though my cheeks are wet with tears, knowing what I am about to do will be the most difficult act I will face.

I walk in further, one more deep breath, removing the lid. Slowly I let him go.

I can't look back as his ashes float out to sea.

'Goodbye my love.'

Epilogue

'Auntie, auntie.'

'What is it Alex?'

'Want to hide.'

I point. 'Okay, go and hide behind the big tree.' He runs to the hiding place. 'Who is the bigger kid, your husband Millie or my nephew?'

'He will never grow up Kate, you should know that better than any of us.'

Making his entrance, 'Here I come, ready or not.'

I can see Alex's fair hair, bobbing in out, he hasn't quite got the hang of being hidden yet. He is only 2 years old after all.

'Where is he, I can't see him anywhere.' Jack holds his hand to his forehead, searching.

A little snigger is heard.

Jack makes his move and approaches the tree. 'Here he is.' He picks up his son, the pair of them laughing, joining us at the table.

'This sounds like fun, what am I missing?' My heart still races when I hear his voice.

I turn to face him, in his hand a bunch of red carnations. It's the anniversary of our first date. Alex runs towards George and he ruffles the little boy's hair.

George looks at Jack. 'Mind if I whisk your sister off?'

I get up from my chair and follow George as he heads towards the olive trees, the flowers still in his hand.

'Have you had a good day?' he asks.

'Yes, Alex is keeping us all entertained.'

George smiles. 'He's a lively one.'

'I have some very good news, I was going to tell you later at dinner.'

'Well don't keep me in suspense.'

'I have a buyer confirmed for my house.'

'Great, its been empty for far too long.' George winks at me.

'Remember the first time you brought me here.'

'How can I forget. You put the whole grape in your mouth and tried to keep composed.'

'You could have warned me.'

'It was just about here, if I remember.' He put his free hand in mine, teasing me between the trees. 'I didn't get a kiss that time.'

'Who says you are going to this time?' He leant in for his kiss and I let him have his way.

George pulled back and then he dropped down on one knee. 'Kate, will you do the honour of marrying me?'

'I thought you'd never ask.'

ABOUT THE AUTHOR

Andrea Stallan

Andrea lives in Coventry with her husband and two teenage sons.
This is her debut novel.

Printed in Great Britain
by Amazon